LOVESTRUCK

It was two-thirty in the morning, and his composition was due in a few hours. If Ken didn't hand it in, he'd fail English and be thrown off the football team. When that happened, how would Suzanne feel about him? Would she still love him? The answer was pretty clear in Ken's head. When all this came out, Suzanne would dump him for sure, no matter what she'd said.

He glanced at Elizabeth's paper. It was so easy for her. She wrote these stories for fun. She didn't hand them in to anyone, no one was forcing her to write them. She hadn't even ever showed one to anyone. If only the paper in front of him were his and not Elizabeth's, everything would be fine. If only the title page had Ken Matthews written on it. . . .

Bantam Books in the Sweet Valley High Series
Ask your bookseller for the books you have missed

SWEET VALLEY HIGH

LOVESTRUCK

Written by
Kate William

Created by
FRANCINE PASCAL

BANTAM BOOKS
TORONTO • NEW YORK • LONDON • SYDNEY • AUCKLAND

RL6, IL age 12 and up

LOVESTRUCK
A Bantam Book / March 1986

Sweet Valley High is a trademark of Francine Pascal

Conceived by Francine Pascal

Produced by Cloverdale Press Inc.,
133 Fifth Avenue, New York, N.Y. 10003

Cover art by James Mathewuse

ISBN 0-553-25471-5

Published simultaneously in the United States and Canada

To Rodney Vaccaro

One

Elizabeth Wakefield sat by the family pool in the bright Sweet Valley, California, sun, trying desperately to drown out her twin sister's voice. Jessica was talking about the centennial student picnic again. Though Bruce Patman, president of the Sweet Valley Centennial Student Committee, had put her in charge of the picnic more than two weeks ago, now that the day of the celebration was approaching, it was all Jessica talked about. It wasn't that Elizabeth wasn't interested in Sweet Valley's centennial. Of course she was. Everyone was. It was going to be a huge celebration with a parade, fireworks, special exhibits, an exhibition football game, and the picnic. Nearly everyone in Sweet Valley was involved in one way or another, but to Elizabeth,

1

it sounded as if Jessica thought the picnic was the only event.

Although it was only four in the afternoon, Elizabeth felt absolutely exhausted. It seemed as though she hadn't slept for a month. Just a week before, Elizabeth, her sister, and their friends Bruce Patman and Nicholas Morrow had spent all their waking hours trying to rescue Nicholas's family from the couple who had kidnapped them. Phillip Denson, a deranged former employee at Mr. Morrow's computer firm, had held Mr. and Mrs. Morrow hostage in his house, while Denson's friend, Claire, stood guard over Nicholas's sister, Regina, at the Morrow estate. Day after day had gone by as the Wakefield twins, Nicholas, and Bruce waited for an opportunity to rescue the Morrows. Finally the four friends devised a daring plot to free Regina and her parents at the same time, and to foil the kidnappers.

The strain of the Morrow kidnappings had caught up with Elizabeth, and she had been resting a good deal throughout the previous week. Today she had been looking forward to a few quiet hours by the pool. But just as she had lain down in a chaise longue, Jessica had come outside. Elizabeth had tried to avoid answering her twin's questions by wrapping her beach towel around her ears. When she realized that it wasn't working, Elizabeth had dived into the pool and stayed under water for almost a full minute in the hope that Jessica would go away. But it was to no avail: Jessica was on a roll. Giving up, Elizabeth had climbed out of the pool and was now sitting by the edge of it, dangling her feet in the water.

"Maybe we should think about hiring a band," Jessica went on. "It'd take money away from the final profit, but live music is so much better than records, don't you think? Of course, I'd like to get The Droids to play, but they might be busy that weekend."

Elizabeth looked up at her sister. It was like looking in a mirror. Both twins were blessed with the same sun-streaked blond hair and the same blue-green eyes, and each had a little dimple on her left cheek. Everything about the twins' appearance was identical—down to the matching gold lavalieres they both wore, presents from their parents for their sixteenth birthday. But there the similarity ended.

Elizabeth had always been the sensible twin. She was a good student, loved to read and write, and was a sweet, sincere, and friendly person. Elizabeth could always be counted on to do what was right. Jessica, on the other hand, seemed at times to care only about herself and having fun. She loved adventure, good-looking boys, and wild clothes. Jessica's search for a good time had often gotten her into trouble and many times

Jessica had counted on her twin to help clear things up. But Elizabeth never faltered in her devotion to Jessica. No matter how much trouble Jessica stirred up, Elizabeth's loyalty was always to her twin.

Jessica was sitting on a chair on the patio that surrounded the pool. "Of course," she said, "I suppose the important thing is to raise money for the community. But who's going to care about that if no one's having a good time?"

Elizabeth sighed loudly. She thought that if she heard one more word from Jessica about the centennial picnic, she would explode. From the day Jessica had been put in charge, she had been driving everyone in her family crazy. If she wasn't persuading someone to do something, she was throwing out hundreds of ideas, pretending to be asking for advice. *As if Jessica ever takes advice from anyone*! Elizabeth thought.

"Well," Elizabeth offered, "do you have enough money in the budget to cover a band?"

"I think so," Jessica replied uncertainly. "But I'd hate to dip too much into the profits. That's the good thing about records. I could borrow them, so they wouldn't cost anything."

Elizabeth swung her legs out of the water and stood up. "Well, maybe you can get The Droids to do it for free." Elizabeth knew Dana Larson, the lead singer for The Droids, and Emily Mayer, their drummer, pretty well. She

4

was sure the band would pitch in and help if it could.

"That's a great idea. Wait until I tell Lila!" Jessica smiled.

"Jess," Elizabeth warned, lying down on one of the chaise longues on the patio surrounding the pool, "don't count your Droids before they hatch. They might have a paying job that day. Remember?"

Jessica began toying with a strand of her sun-streaked hair. "Don't be silly, Liz. Everyone who's anyone is going to be at that picnic. Either as a paying guest or. . . ." Jessica smiled at her sister. It was that too-sweet smile that Jessica used when she wanted a favor from her twin.

Elizabeth moaned. "OK, Jess. What do you want me to do?"

Jessica jumped up from her chair and dropped down at the foot of Elizabeth's chaise. "Well, it'd be a big help if you'd man the kissing booth. After all, you're the most logical choice. What guy in Sweet Valley wouldn't pay a dollar to give Jessica Wakefield's twin a kiss?"

"Jess, your humility amazes me," Elizabeth said, giggling. "But actually, that job doesn't sound bad. All right, I'll do it."

"Great!" Jessica jumped to her feet. "Do you think you could also write the copy for the posters? You know you're so much better at that sort of thing than I am," Jessica said in her most flattering tone. "By the way, do you have any ideas for decorations? I just can't figure out what to do. I mean, there's nothing out there but a bunch of trees. It isn't like we're going to be in the gym or anything."

"Wait a minute," Elizabeth said, sitting up. "Just what are *you* going to do?"

"I'm the chairperson," Jessica said haughtily. "Half the job is delegation. Dad says that all the time."

"Yeah? Well, what are you delegating yourself to do?" Elizabeth asked.

Jessica ran her fingers through her hair. "Liz, I can't take care of everything."

Elizabeth stared at her sister. "What I am trying to get at, dear sister, is, if I do the posters and the kissing booth and the decorations, what's left for you and Lila?"

"OK," Jessica said sullenly, "I guess I could give some of that stuff to Lila. I mean, she *is* supposed to be my assistant."

Elizabeth smiled at the thought of Lila Fowler being Jessica's assistant. One of the richest girls in Sweet Valley, Lila was as beautiful and popular as Jessica. Even though the two of them were best friends, they were often at each other's throats about something. "Does Lila know she's your assistant?" Elizabeth asked.

Jessica's expression was sheepish. "Well,

that's not exactly how I phrased it when I asked her."

"I can imagine," Elizabeth said, smiling. She knew that Lila was too much of a snob to be anyone's assistant. Elizabeth was certain Jessica had given the job a much more impressive title, or Lila would never have accepted.

Suddenly Jessica looked very serious. "I don't think you've grasped the importance of this event, Liz," she said. "I mean, a centennial only comes along once every hundred years. A hundred years, Liz! And I've been put in charge of a major charity event. This is a big responsibility. It's an event that people will be talking about for years."

"Raising money for the community is a wonderful thing, Jess, but I don't think it's going to win you a Nobel Prize."

"I don't expect a prize, Liz," Jessica said in her best hurt voice. "Just the thought of raising money for a good cause is enough for me."

I'll bet, Elizabeth thought to herself. She knew it was awful to think that way about her twin sister. But Elizabeth knew Jessica seldom did anything for anyone other than herself. But whatever Jessica's motivations for doing a good job of organizing the picnic, Elizabeth had to admit it was for a good cause.

Elizabeth smiled. "Jess, I'd be happy to help you with anything you need."

"Elizabeth Wakefield, you are the best sister any girl ever had."

"*But*," Elizabeth added, "I can't take care of the decorations. That's a lot of work, and I'm already overloaded with the special edition of *The Oracle*." *The Oracle* was Sweet Valley High's newspaper. Elizabeth wrote the "Eyes and Ears" column, as well as articles on a variety of subjects.

The smile on Jessica's face faded, and she looked thoughtful. "OK, I guess that's all right. I can get Lila to take care of that. But you'll do the kissing booth and write the poster copy, right?"

"Sure," Elizabeth said. She turned as she heard the hiss of the sliding door leading into the house. Mrs. Wakefield came out onto the patio. She was wearing a blue terrycloth cover-up over her white, two-piece swimsuit. Elizabeth smiled as she looked at her mother. With her tanned, youthful figure and her blond hair, Alice Wakefield was sometimes mistaken for the twins' older sister. Mrs. Wakefield looked especially beautiful that day, Elizabeth reflected, probably because she had had a chance to relax, having taken a day off. Mrs. Wakefield was an interior designer and lately had had an unusually busy schedule.

"Well, if it isn't 'double trouble,' " she said and laughed, looking at the twins.

Jessica moaned. "*Honestly*, Mother. I hate it when people say that."

8

Elizabeth eyed her sister and said, " 'Single trouble and sister' might be more accurate." Then she laughed.

Jessica stuck her tongue out at Elizabeth.

Mrs. Wakefield dropped a towel on one of the lawn chairs and turned to the twins. "So, what's on the agenda for this afternoon? More daring rescues? Foiling an assassination plot? Or are you two just going to try something simple, like taking over a small country?"

Elizabeth sat back in the chaise and closed her eyes. "I think we've had our fill of adventure for a while."

"You said it," Jessica agreed. "Anyway, I'm too busy with this picnic to get involved with anything else."

Their mother started the stretches that preceded her daily swim. "That's right. How's it going?"

"Terrific," Jessica stated. "But there's just so much to do!"

"That's the way those things are," her mother said sympathetically.

"Fortunately," Jessica added, "I have a wonderful sister, who's helping me out." Jessica smiled at Elizabeth. "If everything goes as planned, the picnic should be the high point of the whole celebration."

"We might need it if Sweet Valley doesn't win the football game," Elizabeth said thoughtfully.

"Why do you say that?" Mrs. Wakefield asked.

Elizabeth sighed. "Well, it seems that having Ken Matthews playing is crucial to our winning. Without him as quarterback, we haven't got a chance, and it looks as though he might not be in the game."

Her mother stopped stretching and sat down on the end of Elizabeth's chaise. "Oh, really? Why's that?"

"Well—" Elizabeth began, but Jessica, always eager to gossip, burst in excitedly.

"Ken is failing English. English! Can you believe it? And if he gets a failing grade, they won't let him play."

"I see," Mrs. Wakefield said thoughtfully.

"It's going to ruin the whole afternoon if we lose," Jessica moaned. "And then, all this work I did on the picnic will be for nothing."

"Well, there's still a chance," Elizabeth said. "Ken has one more assignment before the game: a short story due Wednesday. And if he gets a good grade on that, he'll be able to play."

"It must be pretty hard for Ken if everyone at school knows about this," Mrs. Wakefield stated.

"Well, not everyone knows. Jess and I found out from Bruce Patman. I don't think many other people are aware of it. It would probably be the best thing for Ken if it stayed that way." Elizabeth eyed her twin warningly.

The three of them were silent for a moment. "You know," Elizabeth said finally, "maybe it wouldn't be a bad idea for me to call Ken and offer to help him, like you suggested, Jess."

"I can't imagine that he isn't getting help already. From Suzanne Hanlon," Jessica said sarcastically. She didn't hide her dislike for Suzanne. To everyone's amazement Suzanne and Ken had recently begun dating each other. Even Elizabeth agreed that they were an unlikely couple. Suzanne was from a very wealthy family and always made a point of demonstrating how cultured and refined she was. Just the week before, she had phoned Elizabeth about a literary evening she was organizing at school for the Honor Society. Ken, on the other hand, was the captain of the Sweet Valley High football team and seemed more at home on the playing field than in a concert hall. But Elizabeth didn't share Jessica's dislike for Suzanne. In fact, she hardly knew her. Elizabeth had to admit that at the few meetings of Pi Beta Alpha she had attended, she had found Suzanne to be aloof and snobby. Pi Beta Alpha was the exclusive sorority that the twins belonged to. But then, everyone there seemed aloof and snobby to Elizabeth. She had joined the sorority at Jessica's insistence and was now a member in name only. Elizabeth figured that if Ken liked Suzanne, that was his business. She only hoped, for Ken's sake, that Suzanne's attraction to him was genuine.

"Ken might be afraid to tell Suzanne about his grade," Elizabeth said, thinking aloud. "After all, it isn't the sort of thing he'd want to broadcast."

"Especially to someone like Suzanne Hanlon," Jessica said slyly.

Elizabeth stood up. "You know, I think I *will* give Ken a call." She checked her watch. It was four-thirty. "He should still be at school. I can probably reach him at the athletic office after practice."

"I think that's a good idea," Mrs. Wakefield agreed. "At least he would appreciate the offer."

Elizabeth slid open the door and went inside the house. She walked into the kitchen, poured herself a glass of iced tea, then sat down by the phone. A few minutes later, the high school office had put her in touch with the athletic office, and she was waiting as the person on the other end called Ken to the phone.

"Hello," Ken said on the other end. He sounded slightly out of breath.

"Hi, Ken. This is Liz Wakefield."

"Oh, hi, Liz," Ken said. He sounded a little puzzled by the call.

Elizabeth picked up a pencil and began

doodling on the pad next to the phone. "I hope I'm not taking you away from anything."

"No," Ken replied. "We just finished practice."

"Good," Elizabeth said. "Ken, I don't know how to put this delicately, so I'm just going to say it. I've heard you're having some trouble in English."

"Who'd you hear that from?" Ken said, sounding annoyed.

"That doesn't matter," Elizabeth replied. She didn't want to get Bruce into trouble with Ken. "I'm calling because I thought I might be able to help. I know the whole situation, and I know about the writing assignment. If you'd like, I'd be glad to give you a hand."

Ken was silent for a moment, and Elizabeth began to think that her idea might not have been such a good one. "Actually, Liz," Ken finally said, "I could use a hand. I don't know why, but I'm just freezing up on this thing. Maybe if we could talk about it, it might help."

"Sure." Elizabeth sighed in relief. "Can you stop by later this afternoon?"

"That would be great," Ken answered. "Just give me about half an hour to shower and get dressed."

"No problem," Elizabeth said. "I'll be here."

"Great. See you in a while," Ken said, sounding much happier than he had a few minutes earlier.

Elizabeth said goodbye and hung up. She picked up her glass and walked out of the kitchen, thinking about Ken. She knew what it could be like to be stuck on something you were writing. Even though she had been writing for years, she sometimes still had problems getting started. Perhaps if she could talk to Ken and show him some things she'd written, it might help him.

Elizabeth walked onto the patio, pulling the sliding glass door shut behind her. Her mother was swimming laps in the pool, and Jessica was sitting by the diving board, paging through an issue of *Vogue*.

"Did you talk to him?" Jessica asked without looking up from the magazine.

"Yes," Elizabeth took her place on the chaise. "He's coming over here in about half an hour."

"Well"—Jessica eyed her twin slyly—"that's quick."

"I swear, Jess," Elizabeth said in a tired voice. She knew what her twin was thinking. Jessica would like nothing better than to have Elizabeth steal Ken from Suzanne. "We're just going to talk about English. You're welcome to stay with us and listen if you like."

Jessica wrinkled her nose. "Stay and listen to an English lecture? No, thanks." She stood up and closed her magazine. "No, I think I'll go in and make some calls. Let me know if anything interesting develops," she called over her shoulder.

Elizabeth watched as her twin disappeared inside the house. Then she sighed and closed her eyes. Thank goodness Jessica had gone away. That would give her a half hour of peace and quiet. She certainly needed it.

Two

Ken Matthews finished tying his sneakers and placed his football helmet in his locker. He ran a hand through his blond hair and sighed deeply. It had been a tough practice.

Preparing for a game against the Palisades Pumas was always rough. Palisades always had one of the best teams in the state, and they were even better now that Peter Straus was playing quarterback. Straus was a senior at Palisades High, and several major colleges had already tried to recruit him. With Straus playing, Ken knew it was essential that he make his best effort in the game. But if he didn't bring up his English grade, it looked as if he wouldn't even be playing.

Ken could sense the pressure his predicament

was putting on the rest of the team. Although they tried not to show it, most of them knew about the English grade and were upset about the possibility that Ken might not play. He could see it in their eyes. They weren't giving up on him, but they were getting ready for the worst.

Ken felt as if he had been living with this pressure all his life, but it had been about two weeks since the meeting with Mr. Collins, his English teacher. Coach Schultz had come up to Ken as he was making his way to the showers after practice and said he'd like to see him in his office. The coach, who was usually friendly and talkative, seemed quiet and even a little angry.

Roger Collins was sitting in the coach's office when they entered, and Ken knew that meant trouble. He knew he had been letting his grades slip, but he didn't think things had gone as far as they had.

Bruce Patman was also there, and that seemed a little strange until Ken remembered that Bruce was the student president of the centennial committee. By that time, it was obvious to Ken what they wanted to see him about.

Mr. Collins outlined the whole program. He had a list of Ken's grades for the semester and talked a lot about his distracted attitude in class. It looked grim.

"You're not dumb, Ken," Mr. Collins stated, in the fair way that had made him a favorite of the students at Sweet Valley High. "That's the whole problem. You're just not working up to your potential. I know football is very important to you, but the main reason you're in school is to learn. We just can't overlook a failing grade and let you continue to play football."

Coach Schultz spoke up. He seemed to be holding back, as if he were really upset and didn't want to show it. "Listen," he began quietly, "we're not talking about just another game here. We're talking about the exhibition game for the centennial. It's going to put a damper on the whole celebration if we lose that game, and we need Ken to win it."

Bruce picked up the coach's argument. "It's just one game, Mr. Collins. Couldn't you just ignore this whole situation for a few weeks? After that, I'm sure Ken would be willing to put in a lot of extra time on his studies. Wouldn't you, Ken?"

"Really, Mr. Collins," Ken said earnestly, "I'd be willing to do just about anything if it means I can play in that game. I didn't mean for my grades to slip this badly—"

"I know you didn't, Ken," the English teacher interrupted him, "but the fact is that they did. The rules are very clear about this, and I can't make an exception. That rule about extracurricular activities and grades is there for a reason. If I make an exception now, it'll look like I'm playing favorites. I just can't do that."

Ken remembered studying Coach Schultz's face. He knew what was going through his mind. The Sweet Valley squad was good, but without Ken they wouldn't be able to beat Palisades High in the exhibition game. Not when Palisades had Peter Straus playing for them. It tore Ken's heart to disappoint the coach. More than losing the game or failing English, he was letting the team down, and that was something he had never thought he'd do.

Mr. Collins smiled. "It isn't hopeless. There *is* that short-story assignment I gave you, which is due Wednesday. If you can pull it off and give me a good paper, Ken, it'll be enough to pass you. If not, we'll have no alternative but to keep you off the team until you bring the grade back up."

A hard slap on his back brought Ken back from his daydream. "Looking real good out there." Ken turned and saw John Pfeifer, the sports editor for *The Oracle*. "You guys are going to make mincemeat out of Palisades."

"Yeah." Ken tried to sound as confident as possible.

"Can't wait to cover that game, Ken. I'm going to make you sound like Hercules in shoulder pads." John laughed and took off.

Sure you will, thought Ken. *But Hercules on the bench might be more like it!*

As he walked down the hall, Ken knew that if he was going to pull this one off, he'd need some help. He had never been any good at writing. For some reason, when he had to pull a whole idea out of his head and develop it, he froze. It was funny. It didn't bother him at all to face a whole line of one-hundred-and-eighty-pounders who wanted his blood, but the sight of a blank sheet of paper gave him chills.

That was why he had gotten so excited when Elizabeth Wakefield had called and offered her help. Everyone knew Elizabeth was a good writer. If anybody could get him on the right track, it would be her.

As Ken walked out the front door of Sweet Valley High and down the steps, he was filled with a strong feeling of hope. With Elizabeth's help, he knew he could pull up his grade.

Suddenly a voice broke into his thoughts. "Well, hello, handsome!"

Ken didn't have to look to know who it was: Suzanne. She was standing next to him, looking just wonderful in a short skirt and a loose-fitting silk pullover that accentuated her willowy figure. She smiled at him. Her hazel eyes seemed to look right through him. A chill raced up Ken's spine. No matter how many times he looked at Suzanne, she still gave him that chill.

Suzanne linked her arm through Ken's. "Are you in a hurry? Father's picking me up in a few minutes. Can you wait?"

"Sure." Ken smiled. He was always amazed at how poised Suzanne was. Ken thought a lot of the kids at Sweet Valley held that against her. They thought she was a snob. But Ken knew differently. He knew how warm and wonderful he felt when he was with her. Just seeing her washed all thoughts and worries about the English assignment right out of his head. When he was with Suzanne, nothing else seemed to matter. "How'd you do on your French quiz?" he asked.

"Oh, it was a breeze." She laughed. "The hardest part was the dictation. It's so difficult for me to understand Ms. Dalton's accent sometimes. She has this northern French accent, and it sounds like ducks quacking."

Ken laughed with Suzanne, even though he had no idea what she was talking about. All French sounded the same to him, but if there was a difference, he knew that Suzanne would know.

"I was hoping practice would be over soon," Suzanne said.

Ken knew Suzanne wasn't a big football fan. Unlike most of the other kids he knew, Suzanne hardly even went to any of the games.

"I know this is short notice," she went on,

"but I was wondering if you'd like to come by for dinner tonight. It won't be any big deal, just my parents and my brother, but I thought it might be fun. You've never really met them."

"I know," Ken agreed. He frowned slightly as he remembered the English assignment. He knew he should stay home and work on that, but as quickly as it came, the thought went away. He had plenty of time to work on the paper, and with Elizabeth Wakefield helping him, Ken was sure he could pull it off. Besides, even though she said it wasn't, Ken felt his meeting her parents was important to Suzanne.

"We can't make it a late night," Suzanne went on. "I've still got so much to do for the literary evening. Oh, by the way, Elizabeth Wakefield has agreed to read a poem of hers. Isn't that great?"

"Yeah, great," Ken agreed. He felt a little guilty that he hadn't told Suzanne about Elizabeth's offer to help him, but he was sure Suzanne didn't know about his problem, and he wanted to keep it from her for as long as possible. It wasn't something he was proud of.

"Of course, if you've got something else planned tonight—"

"No. I'd love to come," Ken interrupted.

Suzanne beamed at him. "Good. I'm so glad."

Just then a Rolls-Royce drove into the parking

lot. Suzanne turned away from Ken. "Whoops. There's my ride."

"Nice car," Ken said as he looked over the sleek Silver Shadow. "What does your dad drive when he wants to impress people?"

"Oh, he takes the newer Rolls. This one's our second car." Suzanne winked at Ken and kissed him quickly. "See you tonight. Seven-thirty."

"I'll be there." Ken watched Suzanne bounce down the stairs, her short, silky brown hair gleaming in the sun. She climbed into the front seat. He waved as the Rolls pulled away.

Ken's thoughts turned gloomy again as he walked to the white Toyota his parents had helped him buy the summer before. He loved being with Suzanne. Even though he had never been particularly interested in classical music and art, he loved the way she talked about them. She was always so full of passion. She also loved to talk about literature. What would she think if she found out he was flunking English? He had to pass that class. He couldn't let Suzanne down. He couldn't.

Some of the gloom started to leave Ken as he turned the key in the ignition, threw his car into gear, and headed for the Wakefield home. He switched on the cassette deck, and a Mozart symphony rang from the speakers. Ken smiled.

At Suzanne's suggestion the two of them had gone to hear the Sweet Valley College orchestra play an evening of Mozart the previous week. Afterward Suzanne had presented Ken with the cassette. At the time Ken had appeared grateful, but secretly he was disappointed. Although he had told Suzanne he had enjoyed the concert, Ken had had to struggle to stay awake.

Of course, whenever Suzanne had ridden in his car with him, Ken had played the tape and said how much he liked it. There wasn't anything wrong with that, was there? After all, he didn't want her to think he didn't appreciate her gift. Trying to like the things your girlfriend liked was what being in love was all about. If he didn't like the things she did, there was no harm in being a little flexible. Ken didn't want a single problem to mar his relationship with Suzanne.

As he stopped at a traffic light, Ken sighed and pressed the Eject button on the cassette deck. The Mozart tape popped out, and Ken put it on the dashboard. He leaned over, opened the glove compartment, and chose another tape. As the light turned green, the raucous sounds of the Rolling Stones began to blast from the speakers.

Ken knew Suzanne would disapprove. She had told him once that she thought rock music was for people without any taste at all. He wondered what she would say if he presented her with a tape by Mick Jagger. At first, the thought of her reaction caused Ken to smile, but as he contemplated it, his smile faded. He couldn't imagine Suzanne agreeing to listen to rock music or to do anything just because he liked to. Ken didn't mind listening to Mozart once in a while, but he wanted Suzanne to try to like some of the things that were important to him. As long as he and Suzanne were together, they would never go to the Beach Disco or a rock concert.

Then Ken pictured Suzanne as he last saw her, a broad smile lighting her face as she greeted him on the front steps of Sweet Valley High. As long as he could be with Suzanne, he would gladly give up almost anything. She was the most important thing that had ever happened in his life.

Three

"Liz!" Elizabeth heard her mother's voice calling her from the back of the house. Without realizing it, she had fallen fast asleep.

She sat up and rubbed her eyes. "Yes, Mom," she called back.

"Ken Matthews is here."

Elizabeth adjusted the straps on her bathing suit. She smoothed her hair, got up, and walked into the house. Ken was standing in the kitchen, talking to Jessica. "Hi, Ken," Elizabeth said brightly.

Ken smiled. "Hi."

Jessica put her arm around Ken and smiled broadly. "Guess what, Liz? Ken has just agreed to help me out on the picnic."

"That's great, Ken," Elizabeth replied.

"Would you like some iced tea or a Coke or something?"

"Iced tea would be great," Ken replied.

As Elizabeth pulled out two glasses, she thought to herself that Ken looked worried and tired. She could just imagine how he felt. It was hard enough having a bad grade, but to have everyone putting pressure on you to bring that grade up must be tough.

Elizabeth poured the tea over ice cubes and handed Ken a glass. He thanked her and took a long sip. "Boy, I'm thirsty," he said and smiled. "We had a really hard practice today."

"I can imagine," Jessica said. "The big game isn't so far away."

The mention of the game cast a hush over the room.

"Oh, well," Jessica said, "me and my big mouth."

"It's OK, Jess," Ken protested. "That's why I'm here, to talk about it."

"I know you can pull that grade up, Ken," Jessica said brightly. "With old Hemingway Wakefield helping you, you can't miss."

"Thanks, Jess," Ken said honestly.

Elizabeth motioned Ken toward the patio. "Why don't we talk outside? It's such a beautiful day."

"Sure." Ken followed Elizabeth out to the pool and took a chair next to hers.

"So, here's the deal," Ken began. "I've got to bring up this English grade, or I can't play in the exhibition game. Mr. Collins has given me one more chance. You probably already know we've got a short story assignment due. If I can hand in a good paper, I can bring my grade up far enough to pass. But the problem is, Liz, I don't know if I can handle it." Ken sat forward in the chair and put his hands in his lap. "I'm just sort of hung up on this. I just don't have any good ideas. And even if I did, I'm not sure I could pull them together into a decent story. I'm not a very good writer."

Elizabeth really felt bad for him. He looked so sad, sitting there. "I don't know about that, Ken," she said. "I remember some of the other stuff you wrote for class last year, when we were in English together. I remember that report on Edgar Allan Poe that you wrote. I thought it was excellent."

"That was different," Ken replied. "It was just a lot of facts, and I put them in order. It's different for me with a short story. I can get ideas, but I don't know how to fill them out."

"Maybe it might help if you tried reading some good short stories. A lot of times when I'm stuck that's what works for me," Elizabeth offered.

"I've tried that. But it still doesn't help me figure out how to put it all together." Ken slumped down in his chair and slid his hands into his pockets. "If I could just understand how one of those stories was constructed, step by step, I might be able to figure it out."

Suddenly Elizabeth had an idea. "Wait right here," she said. "I'll be right back."

Elizabeth got up from her chair and ran into the house. What Ken had just mentioned about seeing a story from beginning to end had given her a flash of inspiration. She ran upstairs, went into her room, and walked to her work table. She pulled out a folder and studied it for a moment. It would be hard to turn this over to anyone, she thought, but it might just be the thing to help Ken out. She tucked the folder under her arm and ran downstairs and out to the pool.

"Here." She plopped the folder into Ken's lap.

Ken picked it up and leafed through it. "What's this?"

Elizabeth took a deep breath. "It's a short story of mine, complete with all my notes and the outline. It's not so elaborate, and it's only about five pages long. It's a story about a kid who has just moved to Sweet Valley." She watched nervously as Ken paged through the folder. "The story's pretty simple, just about how this boy views the town for the first time, but seeing all my notes and the outline might help you out. You can follow the story from my first idea to the end."

Ken's eyes grew bright. "That's perfect!"

"Ken," Elizabeth went on, "I'd appreciate it if you didn't show this to anyone. I'm a little funny about my short stories. They're very personal to me. I've never shown one to anybody."

Ken looked over the first page of the story. "Why not, Liz?" he asked. "This is really good."

Elizabeth took a breath. "Well, I just—well, I don't want anyone to see any of that kind of writing from me just yet. I hope the story will help you out, but I don't want anyone to see it."

Ken looked at Elizabeth's face. He could tell how much this meant to her, and he was flattered that she would trust him like this. "You bet, Liz. I promise I won't show it to anyone."

"Please," Elizabeth said earnestly. "It may sound silly, but it's important to me."

Ken read a little further. "I can't believe you haven't shown this to anyone," he said. "It's wonderful."

"Well, maybe I will someday. But not right now."

"Don't worry," Ken reassured her. "I'll take good care of it."

Elizabeth stood up. "Come on," she said. "I'll walk you out to your car."

Ken tucked the folder under his arm and followed Elizabeth into the house. Jessica was sitting at the dining room table with Lila Fowler. Lila had a clipboard and was scribbling notes furiously.

"Hi, Ken," Lila said cheerfully. "Hi, Liz."

"Hi, Lila," Elizabeth returned. "I didn't know you were here."

Lila finished writing something on the clipboard. "I just got here."

"What is this?" Ken laughed. "It looks like you're writing a book!"

"Just more planning for the picnic." Lila took a sip from the can of diet soda that sat in front of her. "Honestly, I wouldn't have agreed to be Jessica's co-chairperson if I'd known there was this much to do."

Elizabeth cast a knowing look at her twin, who avoided her glance.

"Ken," Jessica said quickly, "as long as you've offered to help, I was wondering if you'd be interested in manning the girls' kissing booth at the picnic after the game? I really need someone, and after you guys win that game against Palisades, I'm sure every girl in Sweet Valley is going to be dying to give the quarterback a kiss."

For a moment Ken seemed uncomfortable. Then he smiled. "Sure, Jess. I'd be happy to help."

"Oh, that's great!" Jessica squealed. "I'll sign you up for it." She turned to Lila and said in her most businesslike voice, "Did you get that, Lila? Ken will man the kissing booth."

"Right," Lila acknowledged as she wrote it down.

Elizabeth shook her head and left the dining room with Ken. As they walked outside to his car, Ken seemed to slide back into a dark mood. "If I don't bring this grade up, nobody is going to pay two cents for a kiss from me."

"Don't worry, Ken." Elizabeth smiled at him. "You're going to do just fine, both in English and on the football field."

Ken looked at her and smiled boyishly. "You think so?"

Elizabeth winked at him. "I know it."

Ken got behind the wheel of the Toyota and started the engine. "I guess I can't miss with such a great teacher," he said and smiled.

Elizabeth laughed and waved as Ken backed the little white car out of the driveway and drove down the street. Then she walked back into the house and went into the dining room. Lila and Jessica had cleared off their notes, and Jessica had begun to set the table for dinner.

"Are you staying for dinner, Lila?" Elizabeth asked.

"Yes," Lila answered. "Jess and I are going to have to work most of the night on this thing."

"So, how did things go with Ken?" Jessica asked.

"Oh, pretty well." Elizabeth joined in setting the table. "I feel so sorry for him. He's so worried about this thing."

"Well, you can bet on one thing," Lila

responded. "If stuck-up Suzanne Hanlon found out Ken was flunking English, she'd drop him."

"Yeah," Jessica agreed. "It's lucky he came to you for help instead of Suzanne."

Elizabeth pulled the glasses out of the cupboard and began setting them out. "I don't know. Maybe we're being unfair to Suzanne. I mean, none of us knows her very well. She might just be shy."

"Are you kidding, Liz?" Jessica laughed. "If she were any more stuck-up, her feet wouldn't touch the ground."

"Well, there must be more to her, or else Ken wouldn't be interested."

"I don't know," Lila countered. "No matter how nice Ken is, he's still a boy. They're such poor judges of character."

"Lucky for you, Lila," Jessica said and laughed. "If they were any better at it, you'd be home every Saturday night."

"Very funny, Wakefield."

"OK, break it up," Elizabeth said good-naturedly. Even though Lila and Jessica were good friends, Elizabeth sometimes felt like a referee when she was with them. "The important thing is that we help Ken through this so he can get that grade and play in the game."

"Right," Jessica agreed.

"And part of that might be making sure that

everyone doesn't know about it," Elizabeth warned. "Ken doesn't need any more pressure."

"Well, I'm not telling anyone," Lila said, not very convincingly. "I'm not the kind who lives on spreading gossip."

Jessica snorted in reply. Both the twins knew that most nights Lila's phone was as hot as a barbecue grill. Elizabeth could only hope Lila would have some sympathy for Ken and not say anything.

Elizabeth believed in Ken. She was sure that once he set his mind to writing his paper, he'd do a fine job. She still felt a little uncomfortable about letting one of her stories out of her sight, but she knew that if it helped Ken, it was worthwhile.

Four

Suzanne Hanlon's house was high up on the hill overlooking Sweet Valley, where most of the town's wealthy families lived. Even though it was nestled back from the road, surrounded by large trees and shrubs and almost hidden from view, it wasn't hard for Ken to find the house. It was only a short distance from the Morrows' and the Patmans' estates, and Ken had been to both places many times for parties and get-togethers.

Ken drove down the gently curving driveway and arrived at a large courtyard with a spectacular fountain. Facing the courtyard was the house, a huge, white structure that resembled a southern plantation house.

Ken pulled up behind the Rolls-Royce parked in front of the house and turned his engine off.

He checked his hair in the mirror and thought about putting on the tie he had brought with him. The house was formal enough for a tie, but he wasn't sure he should wear it. He was worried it might just make him look dorky. Ken decided against wearing it, got out of the car, and walked up to the front door of the magnificent house.

It gratified Ken that a girl who lived in a house like this could be interested in him. It wasn't that Ken came from a poor family. The Matthewses lived in a comfortable home; Ken had his own car and almost everything else he wanted. But *this* was another world.

Ken rang the door bell. Inside he could hear it chime like the bells in a church steeple. Almost immediately, a man in a dark suit opened the door.

Ken smiled brightly. "Mr. Hanlon? Hi, I'm Ken Matthews."

The man in the suit scowled at him. "My name is Mason, sir. I'm the butler. Miss Hanlon is expecting you. This way, please."

Ken blushed, feeling like a fool. How could he have made such a stupid mistake? He hoped Suzanne didn't find out.

Mason led Ken through a huge foyer to a set of carved mahogany double doors. The butler opened both doors at once and stood aside. Ken got the idea that he was expected to enter the room, so he did. Mason closed the doors behind him, leaving him alone.

Ken looked around. It was like something from a movie. Except for the brightly colored abstract paintings hanging on the walls—some of which Ken thought might as well be hanging upside down—everything in the room was white. The walls, the furniture, the carpeting— all were white. He had never seen a room quite so luxurious or so beautiful.

A door at the other side of the room opened, and Suzanne walked in. She looked so pretty, Ken thought. She was wearing a white sundress that accentuated her perfect tan. "You made it," she said, smiling. "And just on time." She walked to Ken and kissed him lightly on the cheek.

"Gee," Ken said, looking around him. "I feel like I'm in the middle of a blizzard."

Suzanne laughed. "It's something, isn't it? Sometimes I'm sort of afraid to have people over. They get so intimidated."

"It might have something to do with your butler," Ken said. "He's really sort of creepy."

"Oh, Mason," Suzanne replied. "He looks mean, but he's really an old sweetie. When we were little and my brother and I used to play cowboys and Indians, we would always get Mason to be the cowboy. You should have seen him with his silly little cowboy hat on, tied to a tree out back." Suzanne laughed brightly. "I think we have a picture somewhere."

Ken laughed with her. "I'd like to see that." It was difficult for him to imagine someone as stern and solemn-looking as Mason playing cowboys and Indians with two kids.

Suzanne took Ken's hand and led him to the door she had just come through. "Come on, Mom and Dad are out on the sun porch. They're dying to meet you."

"I can imagine," Ken said gloomily. "I should have worn a tie."

Suzanne laughed. "Oh, don't be silly." She smiled at Ken and squeezed his hand tightly before opening the door.

They went into a hall that led onto the sun porch. It was as beautiful as the room they had just been in, but less antiseptic looking. There were lots of plants and big pieces of white wicker furniture. Two couches faced each other in the center of the room. At the far end were a pair of overstuffed chairs with a small table between them. Classical music was playing softly from the stereo against one wall.

Suzanne's father, who had been seated in one of the chairs, stood as Suzanne walked in with Ken.

To Ken, Mr. Hanlon looked as if he had just stepped out of the latest issue of *Gentleman's Quarterly*. He was a tall, slim man with steel-gray hair and a bronze tan. He was wearing a gray cotton sweater and white linen pants.

"Ken, this is my father, Hank," Suzanne said.

Mr. Hanlon shook Ken's hand. "Hi, Ken. It's very nice to meet you."

"It's nice to meet you, Mr. Hanlon," Ken said nervously.

"Oh, you can cut the 'Mr.,' " he said and laughed warmly. "Everyone calls me Hank."

"Hank," Ken echoed uncomfortably. Ken's parents had always insisted that Ken address adults by their surnames. He felt strange calling Mr. Hanlon by his first name.

Suzanne led him to the chair in which her mother sat. Mrs. Hanlon was in her early forties and bore a strong resemblance to Suzanne. They both had dark hair and lithe figures, but Mrs. Hanlon had pale-blue eyes. She reminded Ken of a delicate flower.

"This is my mother, Marian," Suzanne said.

"It's nice to meet you, Marian," Ken repeated uneasily.

Mrs. Hanlon smiled warmly. "We've heard so much about you from Suzanne."

"All good, I hope," Ken said, relaxing.

"Yes." Mrs. Hanlon laughed. "All good." She pointed to the couches. "Why don't we all sit over there? We can talk more easily that way."

Ken sat on a couch next to Suzanne. "Suzanne tells me you're into computers," he said to Mr.

Hanlon, who, with Mrs. Hanlon, sat down on the couch. Immediately he felt self-conscious. *Into computers,* he thought. *What a dumb thing to say.*

Mr. Hanlon smiled. "Yes, I guess you could put it that way. We have a consultant firm that deals with computer layout for major operations."

"That must be interesting," Ken offered.

"Well, it is," Mr. Hanlon replied. "It's a little busy right now. We've just opened another office in San Francisco, and I've been spending a lot of time there."

"How many offices do you have?" Ken asked.

Mr. Hanlon smiled uncomfortably. It seemed to Ken that he really didn't want to talk about business. "Well," he said, "if you count Chicago, which is really just a representatives' station, this will make six. We don't really do any design out of Chicago. That's all done here in Sweet Valley."

"I see," Ken said.

There was an uncomfortable lull. Suzanne's mother broke in. "Ken, you're a junior, right?"

"Yes, that's right," Ken answered.

"Have you thought about what you're going to do after high school?" she asked.

"I'm planning to go to college. I don't know where yet, though."

"Well," Mr. Hanlon said, "you've got time to figure all that out."

The door to the sun porch opened, and Jeffrey, Suzanne's younger brother, entered. He was dressed like his father, in a light sweater and slacks, but he looked a little more rumpled. "I think dinner is ready," he said.

"Jeffrey," Mrs. Hanlon said, "I want you to meet Suzanne's friend, Ken Matthews."

Ken stood up and shook the boy's hand. "Hi, Jeffrey."

"Hi," Jeffrey replied dully, not seeming to care *who* Ken was.

"Well," Suzanne's father said, standing up, "we'd best get to dinner. We're having trout, Ken. I hope that's all right."

"That's great," Ken said.

As they left the room, Suzanne pulled Ken back a little. When they were alone, she smiled at him. "Listen, Ken, I don't think you should mention football at the dinner table."

"Why not?" Ken asked, puzzled.

"Well," Suzanne replied, "Dad doesn't think too much of it. He feels schools focus too much attention on it. It would be better if you didn't talk about it."

"OK," Ken said uneasily. "I understand." But he didn't really understand at all. He realized, however, that it was important for him to make a good impression on Suzanne's father. If Mr.

Hanlon didn't like talking about football, Ken wouldn't say a word about the subject.

"Good," Suzanne said and smiled. "Let's go in."

Ken followed Suzanne down a long hallway into the dining room. It was a large, oak-paneled room with a massive table in the center. The table was large enough to hold ten people easily. The table settings were beautiful. There were large white dishes with delicate flowered borders, antique crystal glasses, and enough silverware at each place to serve a dozen people. When everyone was seated, Mrs. Hanlon rang a small bell on the table next to her. An instant later a young maid brought in the soup. Ken picked up the farthest spoon. He was pleased to notice that everyone else at the table did the same. Silently he thanked his mother for having taught him the proper utensils to use at a formal dinner.

The soup, which was cool, creamy, and delicious, was followed by a beautiful tossed salad. After that, the maid laid a plate of steaming trout in front of each of them. The trout was marinated in fresh herbs and grilled to perfection. The head was still attached, and to Ken the fish looked embarrassed and out of place. *I know how you feel, buddy*, Ken thought to himself.

"Do you fish, Ken?" Mr. Hanlon asked as he lifted a forkful of fish to his mouth.

Ken swallowed his first mouthful of the trout. It had a butter-and-herb taste and just about melted on his tongue. "Yes," Ken replied after swallowing the delicious trout. "My father and I usually go out on the ocean with a charter boat."

Mr. Hanlon nodded. "There's nothing like deep-sea fishing, is there?"

"It's my favorite," Ken agreed. "I caught a small shark last year. We just kept it long enough to take a picture of it; then we tossed it back."

"Mmmm," Mr. Hanlon agreed. "There's no sense in keeping them. Hard to get off the line, aren't they?"

"You said it," Ken took another forkful. "They're just as dangerous out of the water as they are in. This was just a small one, though. Really just a baby."

There was a lull in the conversation. Ken noticed for the first time that everyone was using his knife and fork in a different way from him. Rather than cutting their food and then switching the fork from one hand to the other, the Hanlons cut their food and then piled it onto the back of the fork without changing hands. Ken thought it looked very sophisticated and tried it once, but he couldn't get the trout to stay on the fork. He made a mental note to practice at home.

Mr. Hanlon turned to his son. "How's that Shakespeare assignment coming, Jeffrey?"

The boy made a face into his plate. "Fine, I guess."

"Jeffrey is working on a model of the Globe Theatre as a special project for English," Mr. Hanlon explained. "The Globe was the theatre where Shakespeare put on most of his plays."

Mr. Hanlon's mention of English gave Ken a slight twinge of guilt. But Suzanne did say it had to be an early night for her, he thought. He'd have plenty of time to work on the paper when he got home.

"Do you know much about Shakespeare, Ken?" Mr. Hanlon asked.

Ken put his fork down. "No, I'm afraid not, sir."

"Well, don't worry about it." Mr. Hanlon smiled. "Most kids your age don't care much for it. I might not have either if it hadn't been for my father."

"Here we go," Jeffrey said, looking at Suzanne. It was obvious that this was some sort of family joke.

Mrs. Hanlon spoke from her end of the table. "You see, Ken, Hank's father has a passion for Shakespeare."

"I'll say," Suzanne joined in. "He sometimes gets up from the table at dinner and starts reciting lines from Shakespeare at the top of his lungs."

Her father laughed. "Well, it isn't as if he's a

lunatic. It's usually something that pertains to the dinner conversation."

"We have to watch out," Suzanne said slyly to Ken. "Sometimes Daddy gets started on it, too."

"I do not," Mr. Hanlon said, pretending to be offended.

"You do so," Jeffrey returned.

" 'Oh, how sharper than a serpent's tooth it is to have a thankless child,' " Mr. Hanlon quoted.

Mrs. Hanlon laughed. "There he goes."

"It's from *King Lear*," Mr. Hanlon said to Ken.

"Act One," Suzanne intoned.

"Scene Four," Jeffrey added. The whole family burst into laughter as Ken looked on, smiling uncomfortably.

"Well, I don't care what you say," Mr. Hanlon said as the laughter died. "I think it's wonderful."

Suzanne nodded. "I agree."

"It's sad that schools don't spend more time on things like that," her father went on. "It never ceases to amaze me how schools always seem to have plenty of time for things like football and baseball, but real education—forget it. It's as if they think their only purpose is to produce more stupid athletes."

Ken stared silently into his plate. A moment later he looked up to catch Suzanne's eye, but she was still watching her father. If she had disagreed at all with his last remark, she didn't show it. Even after Mr. Hanlon had moved on to another subject, Ken's feelings about what Suzanne's father had said about sports didn't go away. Was it possible that what he had said was true? Was Ken just another dumb jock?

Everything seemed to point to it. He was having a problem passing English, and hardly anyone ever failed English. Maybe football was really the problem. Yet Ken felt as though he was betraying his teammates by thinking these things. Lots of the athletes at Sweet Valley High were also good students. And Ken knew that football had taught him a lot of important things, too, things he could never learn in a classroom. Ken wanted to point these things out to Mr. Hanlon, but he didn't want to argue with him. After all, Suzanne had warned Ken not to mention football at the dinner table. If he broke his word, Suzanne might get angry.

When dinner was over and he had thanked the Hanlons, Ken walked to his car with Suzanne. He had to talk to her about his feelings about football. He had to make her understand. His mind was a jumble of thoughts, and he walked next to her in the driveway in a kind of moody silence.

They walked past the fountain toward Ken's car. It was about nine o'clock, and the sky was still holding the last bits of light. Ken could hear the peaceful splashing of water in the fountain, but it did nothing to ease his mood.

Suzanne was the first one to speak. "What Daddy said at the table upset you, didn't it?" she asked.

Ken nodded. "It isn't like that," he said. "Sports—it isn't all just a bunch of dumb guys bashing one another's brains out. Your father doesn't understand."

Suzanne cupped Ken's face in her hands and pulled him closer to her, kissing him tenderly on the lips. "It's OK," she said softly. "You did fine. It isn't important."

At that moment Suzanne could have told Ken breathing wasn't important and he would have believed her. He still had the feeling that she didn't understand, but it began not to matter to him. It was like that when they were alone.

He took her in his arms and returned the kiss. "I just want to make sure you don't think of me like that," he said. "That I'm a dumb jock." He stared hard into her eyes, trying to see what she was thinking.

Suzanne returned the stare evenly. "Ken, can't you see how I feel about you?"

Ken dropped his head. "It's just that, well, sometimes I feel I'm not smart enough for you."

Suzanne pushed his head up so he was looking straight into her eyes. "Look. Being smart doesn't have anything to do with how many things you know. It has to do with how you think about the things you do know. You've got a great mind. I really think so. And even if you didn't, it wouldn't matter. You're one of the sweetest people I know."

Ken smiled. He felt slightly silly—like a kid who had complained about a monster hiding in the closet. By saying what she had just said, Suzanne had opened the door and showed him there was nothing there. His worries weren't important, nothing was. It would all work out. He would write that English paper and win the game and prove to Mr. Hanlon that jocks aren't as dumb as he thought they were.

Ken slid into his car and rolled down the window. "See you tomorrow?" he asked.

"If I live." Suzanne smiled. "I've still got a ton of calls to make about the poetry reading."

"You'll make it." Ken smiled. He started his car, kissed her once again, and drove away. He could see Suzanne waving to him as he drove the Toyota down the driveway.

At the road, just past the main gate, Ken pulled to a stop and checked both ways before turning onto the street. A few yards to his left, he saw two familiar figures coming toward him. They were Bruce Patman and Regina Morrow.

"Well, Regina," Ken called to them through his open window, "are you out jogging, or is Bruce chasing you again?"

Bruce ran up to the car window. "Chasing her? I'm having a tough time keeping up."

Regina laughed. "That's just because men age so much faster than women."

Ken thought Regina looked terrific. The last time he had seen her was at the big party her parents had given to celebrate their escape from the man who had held them hostage. Ken had thought Regina had looked a bit nervous at the party. But now, Regina looked every bit as beautiful as she had before her ordeal.

"How come you're out jogging so late?" Ken asked them.

Bruce leaned against the side of the car and stretched his legs. "Oh, I'm so busy with the centennial that I can't run in the morning anymore. I've started running after I finish my homework, and Regina decided to tag along."

"Tag along?" Regina laughed, running her fingers through her long, black hair. "I've practically had to carry you the last mile."

Ken still couldn't believe that Regina could actually hear him now. Until recently, when anyone spoke to Regina, he or she had to face her directly so that Regina could lip-read. But the treatments she had been getting in Switzerland had given her almost normal hearing.

"Did you just come from the Hanlons?" Bruce asked, looking up the driveway.

"Yeah." Ken smiled. "I had dinner with them. It was nice."

"Yes," Regina agreed. "They're lovely people."

"How's the English assignment coming?" Bruce asked.

"Oh, fine," Ken said. "I'm going home right now to dig into it."

"Great." Bruce nodded. "Don't let it get to you." He patted Ken on the shoulder and smiled at him.

"I won't," Ken returned.

"Well, we'd better get going." Bruce turned and playfully punched Regina's arm. "Race you back to your house?"

"Sure." Regina laughed. "See you, Ken."

"Yeah, 'bye," Ken returned. "And watch out, Regina. He cheats."

"I do not," Bruce said lightly. He leaned down into a racing stance. "Ready?"

"Ready," Regina returned.

"OK. On three. One, two—" And with that, he took off.

Ken laughed as he watched Regina running after Bruce. "That's not fair," she was yelling.

Ken put his car into gear and turned toward home. When Bruce and Regina first started dating, nobody thought they would last. They were such an unlikely couple. Ken knew a lot of people felt the same way about him and

Suzanne. But Ken's encounter with Bruce and Regina had just shown him that different kinds of people could be in love with each other. And Ken was sure that he was in love with Suzanne and that Suzanne felt strongly about him. *It doesn't matter what other people think,* Ken said to himself as he steered the car around a bend in the road. *We'll show them that this thing between Suzanne and me is real!*

Five

Ken turned on his typewriter and put in a fresh piece of paper. He was ready to begin work. He sat at his desk for a moment, flexed his fingers, and immediately got up again. *No*, he thought to himself as he crossed the room to his reading chair, *we're going to do this right*.

He picked up the file Elizabeth Wakefield had given him and began to read, first the notes and outline, then the story itself. With this as a guide, Ken couldn't miss. Everything seemed so clearly laid out, from the basic notes to a finished story. It was all there.

Ken tried to concentrate on Elizabeth's notes for her story, but gradually he became aware of the low electric hum of his typewriter. The sound was ruining his concentration, making it very hard for him to focus on the page. He found himself having to reread whole sections of the notes. He got up and turned off the machine.

Now the room was absolutely quiet. *Too quiet*, Ken thought. He remembered the math assignment he had been given in school that day. He had meant to get all that done before his dinner with the Hanlons, but he hadn't even begun. Maybe, he thought, he should do his math homework before starting the short story. That way he'd have nothing else to concentrate on, and his mind would really be clear.

Ken got up and went to his desk. He pulled out his math book and spiral notebook and began going through the problems. It was all pretty easy, and he finished in less than a half hour. He looked at the clock: it was ten-thirty. There was still some time to get to the story. He sat down again with Elizabeth's papers and rubbed his eyes. He was a lot more tired than he usually was at this hour. Ken figured it must have been the extra practice that made him feel this way. He smiled as he thought about football practice. The team had tried out some new plays that day, and Ken really thought the squad was coming together just in time for the big game.

Ken started to think about the upcoming game. He closed his eyes and envisioned the bleachers full of fans, all yelling and cheering for Sweet Valley. He saw himself in his uniform, feeling confident. The teams were on the scrimmage line, and Ken called the signals. The center snapped the ball to him, and Ken ran back, looking for a receiver. He saw Scott Trost running for the end zone. Ken cocked his arm back and—

Ken jumped right out of the chair at the sound of the phone. He rushed and picked up the receiver. "Hello," he snapped.

"Well," Suzanne's voice answered him. "Is something wrong? You sound strange."

"No." Ken laughed. "I'm sorry. I was just really tired."

Suzanne laughed. "Listen, I forgot to ask you while you were here, but a group of us is going to see a film tomorrow night, and I would love it if you came along."

A *film*. Ken laughed to himself. Suzanne was probably the only one of his friends who said "film" rather than "movie." "Sure," he said into the phone. "What are we going to see?"

"*The Seventh Seal*. You've seen it before, haven't you? It's a Bergman film."

Ken's mind raced. He was always forgetting movie titles, but he was sure he had never seen this one. "No, I don't think so."

"What?" Suzanne said in disbelief. "I can't believe you've never seen *The Seventh Seal*. It's a classic."

Ken tried to sound as casual as he could. "I must've been busy with something else when it

57

came out. Did it come out last summer? I was a camp counselor then."

"I think it came out in 1957," Suzanne answered quietly.

"Well, that explains it," Ken said. "I was *real* busy in 1957. I don't think I saw a single movie that whole year."

Suzanne laughed. "The film's at eight o'clock, at the Plaza Theatre. Do you want to meet here at seven-thirty?"

Ken caught a glimpse of the sheet of paper in the typewriter. The English paper was due in two days. If he didn't finish it that night, there would be no way he could go to a movie the next day. He knew he should say no, but how could he say no to Suzanne?

"Seven-thirty is fine," he said.

"Good," Suzanne answered. "I'll see you in school."

"You bet." Ken hung up the phone and stared at the paper. He took a deep breath and went back to his reading chair.

It was funny. Ken knew he had read those first pages of Elizabeth's, but he couldn't seem to remember what was on them. He decided to start over. He began to read again, making notes on the yellow legal pad resting on his lap. Slowly he stopped taking notes. He was losing his concentration again. The room was too quiet. Maybe some music would help. He turned on his stereo and sat back in the chair and continued reading. He yawned and stretched his arms over his head. He really *was* tired. He looked down at the page again. The words seemed to swim in front of him. They seemed to dance in time to the music playing in the background.

It seemed that only a few moments had passed before he heard the loud buzzing of his clock radio, which startled him awake. His neck was stiff, and he felt cold and clammy. It wasn't until he shut the alarm off and saw how bright it was outside that he realized he had spent the whole night sleeping in his chair. The pages of Elizabeth's story were scattered on the floor around him. It was Tuesday morning, and the paper was due the next day.

Six

Ken noticed the look he got from Mr. Collins as he tried to sneak into English class a few minutes late. He was thankful that Mr. Collins didn't say anything to him in front of the class. *Boy*, he thought as he slid into his seat, *if you're trying to rack up points with your English teacher, this isn't the way to do it.*

Mr. Collins was in the middle of giving last-minute instructions on the assignment that was due the next day. "I hope you haven't tried to get too fancy on this one," he was saying, assuming that most students had nearly finished their stories. "Most of the time, especially with creative writing, less is indeed more. When you review your writing, make sure you've said what you want as simply as you could. Make sure your composition doesn't sound as if you wrote with a thesaurus in your lap. This story is a big part of your grade, so I want you all to do the best job you can. Now, let's turn to the reading you had for today and talk about that."

The rest of the class went by in sort of a haze for Ken. He didn't offer anything during the discussion, but he did manage to come up with answers when called on. When the final bell rang, he felt very relieved.

"Ken," Mr. Collins called to him as he was picking up his books. "I'd like to talk to you for a minute."

A feeling of dread passed through Ken as he watched the rest of the class file out. He walked to the front of the room and stood by Mr. Collins's desk. After everyone was gone, the English teacher spoke.

"You were late to class today, Ken."

"I know, Mr. Collins," Ken answered. "I guess I'm moving a little slowly today. I was up pretty late, working on this paper." Ken couldn't tell Mr. Collins that he hadn't written even one word of the story.

"Well, I appreciate your dedication," Mr. Collins said and smiled. "But I don't want you burning yourself out. Make sure to get some sleep tonight, OK?"

"Sure." Ken returned the smile. But he knew there wasn't much chance of his sleeping that night. Not with having to write his short story and going to the movie with Suzanne. He thought he could start the paper right after football practice. That would give him about three hours before he had to pick up Suzanne, and he would still have another couple of hours when he got home that evening after the movie.

"Is that all, Mr. Collins?" Ken asked.

"Yes. That's it. Thanks, Ken."

Ken started out the door. He stopped and turned to face the teacher. "Mr. Collins?"

"Yes, Ken?"

"I just wanted to say thanks for giving me a chance on this. I won't let you down."

Mr. Collins smiled. "I know you won't, Ken."

Ken returned the smile and walked out of the classroom.

"Hey, Matthews, think fast!" Ken turned just as Scott Trost, the main receiver for the Gladiators, passed a football right to his chest. The football hit Ken and rolled in a wobble around his feet. "Lucky for us you're a quarterback and not a receiver," Scott said with a laugh. A sophomore, Scott was a six-footer, with brown hair and flashing blue eyes. He was also on the track team and, because of his speed, was one of the best receivers Ken had ever played with.

"Real funny." Ken sneered as he picked up the ball and tossed it back to Scott. "If you were as quick on the field as you are with your jokes, I wouldn't have to work so hard out there."

"You work hard?" Scott laughed. "All you have to do is stand back and toss the ball. I'm the one who has to run my tail off to catch it."

"Yeah, tossing the ball is the easy part," Ken agreed. "It's the two-hundred-pound killer linemen coming at me who make it a little difficult."

Scott laughed as they rounded the corner. Suzanne was standing at her locker a little way down the hall from them. She didn't see him, however. Watching her, Ken caught his breath. No matter how many times he saw her, he always felt as if the wind had been knocked out of him. Suzanne looked especially beautiful that morning.

Scott studied Ken's face for a moment. "How're you and the lucky lady getting along anyway?"

"Great," Ken replied.

"It's sort of strange." Scott leaned against the lockers and began passing the football back from hand to hand. "I mean, who would have ever figured you two as a couple?"

Ken got a little irritated. He was sick and tired of everyone pointing out how different from each other he and Suzanne were. "Well, don't worry about it so much," he said angrily. "OK?"

"Sure," Scott returned. "I didn't mean anything by it."

Ken's irritation was replaced by a slight twinge of guilt at having yelled at a teammate. He smiled. "It's OK. Sorry I snapped at you."

Scott returned the smile. "Sure thing."

They walked toward Suzanne. Ken smiled brightly and called hello to her.

"Hi, handsome." She smiled in return. "I was hoping I'd run into you."

"What's up?" Ken hoped something else had come up and that she was canceling the movie.

Suzanne closed her locker and walked up to him. "Tonight, before we go to the film, a few of us are meeting for dinner. I was sure you'd want to join us."

"Of course I do," Ken said without thinking. He smiled uncertainly. "What time?"

"Around six?"

A gloomy feeling came over him as he realized that would only leave him about an hour and a half to work on the short story before going out. Ken knew he should say no, but as he looked at Suzanne's smile, he knew he couldn't.

"Sure. Six is fine."

"Good." Suzanne smiled. "I'll see you later then."

"OK." Ken gave her a quick kiss. "See you later."

He and Scott watched as Suzanne ran off down the hall. It was Scott who spoke first.

"She's really something." He gave Ken a

knowing wink. Ken didn't make any acknowl-edgment. He was too busy thinking about hav-ing to stay up all night to finish the paper. "Oh," Scott went on. "Coach said that practice might run a little late today. He really wants to get down that new end play."

Great, Ken thought. *That's all I need.* "OK," he said to Scott, "I'll see you there."

"Terrific." Scott started off toward his next class. "Catch you later."

"Yeah. Later."

Ken stood in the hall for a moment after Scott had walked away. He felt as if he had a two-hundred-pound weight on his back. He couldn't believe that his short story was due the next morning and he hadn't even started working on it.

Ken was so deep in thought he didn't even see Elizabeth until she spoke to him.

"Hi, Ken!"

Elizabeth was with Enid Rollins, her best friend. "Oh, hi, Liz. I'm sorry," he said. "I guess I'm not really awake this morning. Hi, Enid."

"Hi, Ken," Enid returned.

Elizabeth smiled. "How's the story coming?"

"Oh . . ." Ken hedged. "It's coming along."

Enid laughed. Her section of English had been given the same assignment. "I'm glad I started working on it early," she said. "It was really slow going for me. We can't all be natural writers." She nodded toward Elizabeth and smiled.

"Oh, Enid," Elizabeth replied. "Nobody's a *natural* writer."

"No?" she returned. "Well, it seems to come as easy as breathing for you."

"No. It's just as hard for me," Elizabeth declared. "I guess I just like doing it."

"By the way," Ken said to Elizabeth, "that stuff you gave me is a big help."

"Great! I'm glad." Elizabeth took a deep breath and turned to Enid and smiled. "Enid, excuse us for a moment." She took Ken by the arm and walked him a few steps away from her friend. "I was wondering. Well . . . you're really the first person to read any of my stories, and I wondered . . . well, I wondered what you thought of it?"

Ken looked down at the floor. He couldn't admit to Elizabeth he hadn't even finished reading her story yet. He knew it wasn't the story. What he had read he thought was wonderful. "Well," he began, "I think it's terrific. I mean, I knew you were a good writer and all, but, really, Liz, that story is wonderful."

Elizabeth beamed at him. "I'm glad you liked it," she said. Just then, the bell rang signaling the beginning of the next class period.

Enid called to Elizabeth from across the hall. "We'd better run, Liz, or we're going to be late."

"OK," Elizabeth called back. She turned back to Ken. "I'd better go."

"Yeah, me, too," Ken replied.

"I can't wait to read your story, Ken," Elizabeth called over her shoulder as she ran off down the hall with Enid.

Yeah, Ken said to himself quietly. *Me, too.*

Seven

No matter how hard Ken stared at the typewriter, he couldn't come up with any ideas. He checked the clock. It was two in the morning. He had been staring at the machine for at least three hours with no results. For some reason, he couldn't get a single word onto the paper.

If I could just get the first line, he thought to himself. *If I could just start, the rest would come easily.*

But even though Ken knew what to write about, he had no idea how to begin. He had read Elizabeth's story a number of times when he had gotten home from football practice. It was titled "The New Kid," and it was even better than he had imagined it would be. The story was about a boy who had moved from New York City to Sweet Valley. It was amazing how Elizabeth had caught the perceptions of the boy. It sounded as if her character was looking at the town for the first time. And Elizabeth's style was just right. She used simple language, and each sentence was crafted to advance the story in as few words as possible. Ken found himself lost in the thoughts of this boy as he walked through the beautiful California town, the loneliness he felt at leaving New York, and his eventual conclusion that Sweet Valley looked like a place where he could be happy. The story was so good Ken hated to put it down, but after he'd read it the third time, he had only a few minutes to get dressed and pick up Suzanne for dinner.

After his date with Suzanne Ken had come back home, read through Elizabeth's notes again, developed his own outline based on her example, sat down at the typewriter, and slid into a solid stop. It was as if his mind were set in concrete.

Just an opening line, he kept repeating in his head. *Just write something, and the rest will follow.*

But it was no use. His mind refused to focus on the story. Ken began to think back on the evening he had just spent with Suzanne. The first part of it had been terrific. It turned out that Suzanne's friends couldn't make it for dinner, so just he and Suzanne had eaten at the Box Tree Café. After that, they had met her friends outside the Plaza Theatre, bought their tickets, and gone inside. The theatre was almost empty. At first Ken had thought it was because it was a Tuesday night, but a few minutes into the movie Ken changed his mind. This movie was unlike anything he had ever seen. First of all the film was in Swedish. There were subtitles, and Ken was glad about that, but the subtitles were white and usually printed over a white part of the screen, so most of the time he couldn't read them. The subtitles he could read just didn't seem to make any sense. In fact nothing any of the characters said or did made sense. There was this character who was always running or playing chess with another character. Then there were all these other characters, and they were also running around a lot. Then there was a priest who came out of nowhere, and in the end all of the characters went dancing. After an hour Ken found that it took all his willpower just to stay awake.

When the movie was over, Ken expected Suzanne and all of her friends to laugh and say how boring it had been. Instead, they were all very quiet, and no one said a word about the film. Later, in Guido's Pizza Palace, Ken sat with Suzanne and her friends. Everyone wanted to talk about how marvelous the film was. At first Ken thought they were joking. But he quickly realized just how serious they were. They talked about every detail of the film as if it were the most important thing in their lives. Ken sat quietly eating pizza and hoping they wouldn't ask him anything. At times, he had the uncomfortable feeling that Suzanne was ashamed of him. He wasn't anything like any of these people.

There was a couple, Allan Partridge and Meg Winters, who were both seniors at Sweet Valley, but Ken knew them by name only. He knew one of the other guys, Paul Larchesi, because he had acted in a lot of the Valley High theater productions, and then there was Mark Andrews.

Mark was a film student at Sweet Valley College. He was very thin and had long, black hair and piercing, dark eyes. Everyone paid attention to every word he said. Ken didn't miss the fact that Mark was trying his best to impress Suzanne. What bugged him was that it seemed to be working.

While comparing the film to other Bergman films, Mark finally turned to Ken. It was the first time he had even acknowledged Ken's existence all evening. "It seems you're bored by all of this," he remarked dryly.

"No," Ken replied, trying to sound intelligent. "I think it's all really interesting. But I've never seen the film before tonight. Which one was Ingrid Bergman?"

Everyone in the group looked at Ken as if he had just landed from another planet. After a long moment Suzanne spoke up. "It's *Ingmar*

Bergman, Ken. He was the director. *Ingrid* Bergman, the actress, wasn't in the film."

Ken could see utter distaste in the condescending look Mark gave him. "Don't worry, Ken," he said. "People make that mistake all the time. The two of them look so much alike."

Everyone laughed, and at first Ken joined in. Slowly the realization that he'd made a fool of himself sunk in. He stole a look at Suzanne, but he couldn't read what she was thinking.

Ken tried to redeem himself as well as he could. "It's always so hard to keep up with movies. There are so many good ones."

Mark looked at him with another condescending look. "I don't know what films *you've* been seeing lately," he said dryly. "Personally, I haven't seen a film made in the last five years that was worth talking about."

"Oh, really?" Ken replied simply. "Maybe you've been going to the wrong ones."

"Maybe I have." Mark sighed. There was something in the tone of his voice that made Ken feel as though he had said something stupid again.

Mark sat very still and stared at him for a moment. "Suzanne tells me you're on the football team at Sweet Valley, Ken."

"Yes, I am," Ken replied. He had the feeling that he was being set up again.

"That must be interesting." Mark looked at the others as if he'd just said something witty.

Ken knew Mark was making fun of him, and he started to defend himself, but Suzanne interrupted. "Oh, Ken doesn't really care about all that," she said. "He just does it to keep in shape."

Ken shifted uncomfortably in his seat. The truth was that he really did care about football. He was a little annoyed with Suzanne for trying to dismiss the subject so easily. But Ken knew he would never be able to explain to these people what he liked about football without sounding shallow. Finally he just gave up and let the conversation drift to another topic.

Afterward Ken had driven Suzanne home. When they were parked outside of Suzanne's house, she asked Ken how he had enjoyed the evening.

"I just don't seem to fit in with your friends too well," he said. "I don't know anything about films and art and stuff. Maybe your father was right. Maybe I am just a dumb jock."

"Don't be silly," she said. "You're not dumb. It's just that your experience has been limited. It's all a matter of exposure. My friends aren't any smarter than you; they've just seen more truly great films. Why, in a couple of months, I'll bet you'll be just as familiar with Bergman's films as they are. Look at how you've taken to Mozart! Just give it time, Ken.''

Ken was about to protest that he didn't want to see any more Bergman films, that he was quite happy with the sort of movies he'd always enjoyed seeing, and that Mozart wasn't exactly his favorite, but just then Suzanne turned his head toward hers and kissed him passionately. That kiss lay to rest whatever uneasiness he felt. A minute later, Suzanne had gone into the house, and Ken was driving home with his head in the clouds.

But now everything was different. It was two-thirty in the morning, and his composition was due in a few hours. If Ken didn't hand it in, he would fail English and be thrown off the football team. When that happened, how would Suzanne feel about him? Would she still love him? The answer was pretty clear in Ken's head. When all this came out, Suzanne would dump him for sure, no matter what she had said.

He glanced at Elizabeth's paper. It was so easy for her. She wrote these stories for fun and didn't have to hand them in to anyone. No one was forcing her to write them. She hadn't even ever showed one to anyone. If only the paper in front of him were his and not Elizabeth's, everything would be fine. If only the title page had Ken Matthews written on it . . .

A plan began to form in Ken's mind. Elizabeth

had said herself that no one had ever seen her story. All Ken had to do was take the story and make one little change on the title page: Just take out the name Elizabeth Wakefield and type in Ken Matthews. No one would ever know that Ken hadn't written the story.

No. He couldn't do it, he thought. Ken knew that if Elizabeth ever found out, she would be furious. Besides, she had said several times that she didn't want anyone to see her work. *But it wouldn't be her work anymore*, Ken thought to himself. *She wouldn't even have to know*. No one would have to know. It was just an English paper. Nobody except Mr. Collins would ever have to see it.

Ken looked at the blank page in the typewriter. Slowly he lay his fingers on the keys and typed: "The New Kid." He returned the carriage and typed a second line: "A Short Story by Ken Matthews."

Ken rolled the page off the platen and held it in his hands. He took Elizabeth's title page off the story and replaced it with his own. He placed the story neatly in his folder and got undressed for bed.

It was funny. Just a few minutes earlier he hadn't been able to keep his eyes open and now, for some reason, he found he couldn't sleep. It was nearly three-thirty in the morning before he drifted off, and then, it felt as if only a few minutes had passed before his clock radio woke him.

Ken got out of bed and went to his window. It was a beautiful day in Sweet Valley. The sun was shining, birds were singing in the trees, and the grass outside was lush and green. But as he picked up the folder containing Elizabeth's story, Ken felt worse than he had ever felt in his life.

Eight

Jessica sat pressed against the passenger door of the twins' red Fiat Spider, drumming her fingers on the notebook in her lap. She was furious. She turned angrily toward Lila Fowler, who was squeezed between the twins in the small convertible. "I can't believe it!" she exclaimed. "I just can't believe it."

Lila smoothed her hair and raised her eyebrows. "I don't know why you're so upset, Jess. It's not that big a deal."

"Not that big a deal!" Jessica shouted. "I've been counting on you as my right hand for this picnic, and now you announce that you're going to New York next week. If that isn't a big deal, I don't know what is!"

"Calm down, Jess," Elizabeth said as she

turned into the Sweet Valley High parking lot. "It's not Lila's fault that her aunt invited her out to visit."

"Oh, Liz," Jessica replied, "don't you see, she's not going because her aunt wants her there. She's going because she wants a new wardrobe."

Lila rummaged through her purse and pulled out a hairbrush. She began running it through her light brown hair. "Don't act so self-righteous, Jessica Wakefield. If you had the chance, you'd do the same thing."

"I would not," Jessica replied defiantly. "Not if my best friend were depending on me."

Elizabeth pulled the car into a parking space in the Sweet Valley High lot and shut the engine off. "Well, Jess, Lila isn't leaving until Friday. The picnic isn't until a week from Saturday, so that still leaves you a whole week. I'm sure Lila can help you out with all the details until she goes."

"Well, actually," Lila said quietly, "I really have a lot to do to get ready for the trip. I'm afraid I won't have a lot of time."

"Lila Fowler!" Jessica yelled. "I am never, ever speaking to you again as long as I live!"

Elizabeth got out of the car, followed by Lila. She winced as Jessica got out and slammed her car door shut. She stomped off across the parking lot, and Lila hurried after her, trying to explain.

Elizabeth smiled. She knew that Jessica would be able to handle the picnic by herself, and that a week after Lila got back from New York, she and Jessica would be best friends again.

Ken pulled his car into a parking space and shut off the ignition. He rubbed his hand over his eyes. He felt as if he hadn't slept in a week. Even worse, he felt the beginning of a headache. He couldn't shake the black feeling that had come over him the night before. But it was too late now. He had decided what to do, and everything was going to be all right. Of course he couldn't let anyone know about it.

Ken heard someone call his name. Turning around, he saw Elizabeth Wakefield walking toward him. He wanted to turn and run away, but Elizabeth had already seen him. Just the sight of her made him feel worse.

Elizabeth called to him again and waved as she walked over to him. "I was hoping I'd see you before first period," she said pleasantly. "I'm dying to know how your story turned out."

Ken's mind went blank. "Huh?" he muttered.

Elizabeth laughed. "Your story. Are you pleased with it?"

Ken instinctively clutched his papers tighter. It

was as though he felt Elizabeth might be able to see what he'd done through the folder. "Yeah. Yeah, I guess so."

Elizabeth waved to Bruce Patman as he ran by and turned back to Ken. "I can't wait to read it. What's it about?"

Ken panicked. He couldn't think. "Well, I feel kind of funny talking about it," he stammered. "I'll let you read it sometime. You understand, don't you?"

"Believe me, I understand." Elizabeth gave him a knowing smile. "By the way, are you done with my paper? It's not that I don't trust you with it, but it's my only copy."

Ken knew he should tell her the truth, give Elizabeth her paper, and take what was coming to him from Mr. Collins. He knew that if he did he would lose Suzanne and let down the whole football squad, but he just couldn't betray Elizabeth. She had been so trusting. He put his hand on the folder and took a deep breath.

Suddenly Jessica burst in between them. Her face was flushed, and she looked very angry. "I can't believe Lila Fowler," she fumed. "I'm furious. *Furious!*"

Elizabeth turned to Ken and explained. "Lila just dropped a bomb on Jessica. She's going to New York next week to visit her aunt and won't be able to help out with the picnic."

Jessica continued to rave. "I'm never speaking to her again! I swear, never again!"

"Take it easy, Jess," Elizabeth said, trying to calm her anxious twin. "Everything will work out."

"While I have to stay in this miserable town, Lila's going to New York to buy out Blooming-dale's!" Jessica exclaimed. "I can't believe it. She's taking the whole picnic and dumping it in my lap."

Elizabeth thought about trying to reason with her sister, but she knew it wouldn't work. When Jessica was like this, she just had to cool off by herself.

"Everything!" Jessica continued. "The decorations, the food, the music—" Suddenly she stopped, then exclaimed, "Oh, my God! The music! I promised Dana I'd get back to her yesterday, and I forgot. Maybe I can catch her this morning."

Jessica turned to Ken. "You're still planning on being in the kissing booth, aren't you, Ken? We're really counting on you."

She's counting on me, Ken thought to himself bitterly. *Everyone is counting on me for everything.* He looked at the twins, and at that moment he knew he couldn't tell Elizabeth the truth. He was just going to have to go through with his plan and hope no one would ever find out about it. "Oh, yeah," he muttered. "Sure. No problem."

"Great." Jessica sighed. "All I need is to have that fall through. At this date I'd have to get someone like Winston Egbert to be in the kissing booth, and we'd end up making about two dollars."

"Well, I'll be there." Ken turned toward Elizabeth but couldn't meet her gaze. He just stared at the ground. "Oh, Liz, about your paper. It was a big help, but I left it at home. I promise I'll get it back to you."

"Don't worry about it, Ken," Elizabeth said. "Are you going to be at the poetry reading tonight?"

Ken nodded silently.

"Good." Elizabeth smiled. "I'll see you there then."

"Right," Ken nodded. "I've got to go now, or I'll be late for class. 'Bye." He walked away quickly, feeling as though he had just stolen something, which he had.

Elizabeth watched as Ken walked into the school. She was proud of him. It must have been hard to write a paper under all that pressure, she thought. "Well," she said to her twin, "it looks like everything's going to be just fine. Ken finished his paper. I'm sure they'll let him play in the game now."

Jessica walked alongside her sister up the stairs that led to the main entrance of Sweet Valley High. "I don't know why everyone is making such a fuss over that stupid game," she declared. "I mean, it's not like it's the most important thing going on that day. I mean, there *is* the picnic. Of course it looks as though I'm going to have to set that up all by myself . . ."

Elizabeth knew where this was leading. Jessica had already asked her three times if she could help set up the picnic, and Elizabeth had told her three times that she just couldn't. She was writing an article on the centennial celebration for *The Oracle*, and it was crucial that she be at the football game. "Jess, I've already told you—"

"I know, I know." Jessica interrupted. "You have to write another article for that stupid old paper. *The Oracle* is all that really matters to you anyway, Liz. Even when your own sister needs you in a matter of life and death."

Elizabeth stopped walking and faced her twin. "It is hardly a matter of life and death, Jess."

"Oh, no?" Jessica countered. "It's only a major event, and the whole thing is on my shoulders. I swear, I'm never talking to Lila again as long as I live. Except"—Jessica's tone changed as something else occurred to her—"there's this sweater that I saw in a magazine, and I bet they sell it in New York. Maybe while Lila's there, she could pick it up for me."

Elizabeth smiled at the change in her sister. Jessica was always unforgiving until she needed something. "But after you ask Lila about the sweater, you're never going to speak to her again, right?"

"Absolutely!" Jessica declared.

At that, Elizabeth burst into laughter.

Nine

The literary evening was being held in a small, wood-paneled room off the library at the high school. Elizabeth looked around her as she anxiously awaited her turn to read. There were about twenty-five people in the room, seated in three semicircular rows around a small podium. Elizabeth was happy for Suzanne that there had been such a good turnout, but she wondered whether it was because of the readings or because there wasn't much else to do on a Wednesday night.

Elizabeth really wasn't friendly with most of the people there. They were students from Sweet Valley High, but most of them were outside of Elizabeth's regular crowd. Olivia Davidson, the arts editor for *The Oracle*, was there, and she had read a short, lovely poem about her grandfather. Winston Egbert had surprised everyone with an amazingly funny series of short poems. In Elizabeth's opinion, most of the rest of the readings left a lot to be desired. One boy, a dark-haired senior named Ted Jenson, had read a very melodramatic short story about the death of a squirrel. Elizabeth tried as well as she could to keep from laughing during the whole thing. Another senior, Joanie Shreeves, was reading at the moment. Joanie was dressed in black. She was reading a poem about the ghost of a woman named Daphne who had been murdered by her husband.

" 'Daphne sighed,' " Joanie read in a passionate voice, " 'as the world, a bright-red apple, split at the center, revealing a core that rained apple-seed tears on the parched soil of her dreams.' "

Elizabeth smiled as she took her eyes off the girl and let her gaze wander around the room. Ken and Suzanne were sitting together at the opposite end of the semicircle. Ken looked as if he shared Elizabeth's opinion about the poem. His face was a mixture of confusion and boredom. Elizabeth was secretly glad she hadn't caught his eye. She was sure that if they looked at each other they would burst out laughing. Suzanne, however, hung on every word Joanie read. She even gasped and nodded her head several times.

Elizabeth worried privately about the two of them, especially Ken. He seemed to be devoted to Suzanne, and she seemed to feel the same way, but it appeared to Elizabeth that Suzanne was always trying to direct him. She seemed to be trying to change a lot of the best parts of Ken. And Elizabeth was afraid that Ken couldn't see it at all.

Elizabeth refocused on Joanie as the girl finished her poem. " 'A life. Her life. The blood. The warmth. Like a baby with a bottle. The sun. The sun.' "

The girl sat down, and the audience, led by Suzanne, burst into applause. Elizabeth began to giggle. She knew how much the poem must have meant to the girl, but it just seemed silly.

"Now," Suzanne said, "our final reader is Elizabeth Wakefield. Many of you may already be familiar with Elizabeth's work for *The Oracle*, but she also writes poetry. She's agreed to share one of her poems with us tonight. Elizabeth?"

The audience clapped politely as Elizabeth stood. She held the paper firmly in front of her and began to read. She had chosen a poem she had written the year before about her mother. She had wanted to create a picture of the effect her mother's friendship had had on her life. The room became especially quiet as Elizabeth read.

She had chosen to write very simply, but the images were strong and touching.

The room was quiet as Elizabeth finished reading and returned to her seat. Then the applause began, soft at first and then full and sincere. Elizabeth exchanged a wink with Ken, who seemed to be applauding louder than anyone.

The reading broke up, and students moved into small circles to discuss the poems they'd heard.

"That was wonderful, Liz," Suzanne said sweetly as she approached her. She was holding Ken's arm tightly.

"It was," Ken agreed. "I never knew you could say so much with so few words."

"Thank you," Elizabeth said shyly.

"This evening has been such a success, maybe we should do it every month," Suzanne said as she looked around the room. "Maybe next time we can get Ken to read something."

"Oh, I can't write like this," Ken said.

"Sure you can," Suzanne prodded him. "It just takes a little patience. If you put the same time into writing that you do into football, you could really do something wonderful."

Elizabeth noticed Ken's discomfort. He had suddenly lost his smile and become quiet. This was an example of the kind of thing Elizabeth had been thinking about.

"Maybe you could combine the two,"

Elizabeth suggested, trying to be helpful. "There are a lot of good sports poems."

"Oh, Liz, be serious." Suzanne laughed. "Surely there are more important things to write about."

Jessica is right, Elizabeth thought to herself, *Suzanne really is a snob*.

"Excuse me a minute," Suzanne said. As she began walking away, she called out, "Joanie, your poem was so inspired!"

Elizabeth and Ken watched as Suzanne lavished praise on Joanie. "Did you understand one word she said?" Ken asked Elizabeth under his breath.

"No," Elizabeth whispered in return, then smiled.

"Thank goodness." Ken laughed. "I thought I was crazy."

"You must feel pretty good tonight," she said, changing the subject. "I mean, getting your story in and all."

Ken's smile disappeared, "Yeah. I feel OK," he said and began to look around the room uncomfortably. "I'd better get back to Suzanne."

"Sure," Elizabeth said.

Ken nodded to her and walked away. Elizabeth watched him as he returned to Suzanne's side. Ken's modesty about his story puzzled her. She had never figured Ken to be so sensitive about his schoolwork. But she could understand, Elizabeth reflected. After all, if Ken had written something he felt very deeply about, it was perfectly natural for him not to want to talk about it. But as hard as she tried, Elizabeth couldn't shake the feeling that something more was responsible for Ken's strange reaction.

Ten

Liz sat at her desk in the *Oracle* office, rereading her latest "Eyes and Ears" column. Most of the centennial issue had been finished, and Elizabeth thought it looked really good. There was an interview with Coach Schultz on the big game by John Pfeifer, several articles by Penny Ayala on local events, including the picnic and the parade, an article on the history of Sweet Valley by Mr. Fellows, a history teacher, the "Eyes and Ears" column, and a really nice piece by Olivia Davidson on the new mural in the post office, which had been donated to the city by Henry Patman in honor of the centennial. All in all, Elizabeth thought it was one of the best issues they had ever done.

A typo in the first paragraph of her column

caught Elizabeth's eye, and she made the correction in red in the margin. Just then Jessica burst into the office. She looked close to tears. Her voice was quavering, and her face was flushed. "Liz, you have to help me," she cried. "This is a disaster! A disaster!"

Elizabeth looked up at her sister. She noticed that Jessica's hair was out of place. *It really must be something serious*, Elizabeth thought. "Tell me what happened," she said.

Jessica collapsed into a chair near Elizabeth's desk and placed a piece of white cardboard in front of her twin. "I just picked up the posters from the printer's. Look!"

Elizabeth scanned the poster. It was a drawing of several large balloons and party favors. The student picnic, along with information about its time, place, and date, was announced in bright letters in the balloons. Olivia Davidson had drawn the picture, and Elizabeth had written the copy. Elizabeth handed the poster back to her twin. "It looks great," she said.

Jessica rolled her eyes and slapped the poster with the back of her hand. "Great?" she shrieked. "The date is wrong. It's supposed to say the third, but the poster says the fourth. Everything's ruined!"

Elizabeth looked more carefully at the poster. This time she saw the error. "Why can't you just have it changed?" she asked.

"The printer can't get them done in time," Jessica moaned. "They have to be put up today, or no one will see them."

Because of her dealings with *The Oracle*, Elizabeth had had a lot of contact with Ned Fulbright, the man who owned Valley Printing. She knew if Mr. Fulbright had made a mistake, he would certainly fix it. "Well, he should be willing to do something about it," she said calmly to her twin. "After all, it is his fault, isn't it?"

Jessica looked down at the desk and began nervously twisting a strand of blond hair. "Well, I guess I was looking at the wrong month when I wrote the date down for him."

"Oh, Jess . . ."

Jessica looked up. She had tears in her eyes. "Liz, what am I going to do?"

Jessica didn't cry often, and when she did, it was a sure sign to Elizabeth that it was time for her to take over. She handed Jessica a tissue and patted her hand. "OK. Calm down, Jess." Elizabeth reached into her drawer and pulled out a small bottle. "Here's some correction fluid. Start whiting out the wrong date, and we'll write in the correct date with a felt-tipped pen."

"But there are so many," Jessica complained.

"Well, you'd better get started then," Elizabeth said as she pushed her sister toward a desk across the room. "As soon as I finish proof-reading my column, I'll come over and help."

"OK. Thanks, Liz," Jessica said, sniffling. She sat down meekly at the desk and began correcting the date on the first poster. Elizabeth smiled at her and started back to her desk. She had gotten halfway there when Jessica called out, "As long as you're at your desk, would you mind calling 'Frankly Speaking' to see if Jeremy Frank will give us a public-service plug? Oh, and could you see if the stationery store will deliver the decorations to the park Saturday morning? I won't have any time to pick them up. You're the most wonderful twin sister I've ever had." Jessica smiled sweetly.

Elizabeth thought briefly about pointing out to Jessica that she had other things to do, but she knew it would be to no avail. She shrugged her shoulders and started back to her desk.

Jessica stopped her once again. "Is it all right for me to use the phone? I have to call the caterer."

"Sure," Elizabeth answered.

Elizabeth stayed and listened for a while as Jessica got on the phone with the caterer. She ran down the menu, which sounded wonderful, and ended by agreeing to call them two days before the picnic to confirm the order.

"There, that's done," Jessica said as she set down the phone.

Elizabeth smiled to herself. Jessica really was doing a wonderful job on this picnic. Elizabeth knew how hard it was for her fun-loving twin to keep her mind on details, but Jessica seemed to have things in hand. "Jess?" Elizabeth said to her twin.

Jessica looked up from the poster she had begun working on. "Yes?"

"I just want you to know I'm really proud of you." Elizabeth smiled. "I think you're doing a great job with this picnic so far."

Jessica smiled broadly. "Thanks, Lizzie."

It made Elizabeth feel good whenever Jessica called her Lizzie. She knew it was a special term of affection and one that Jessica reserved for moments when she really felt close to her sister.

Just then the door to the *Oracle* office opened, and Penny Ayala, the editor-in-chief, rushed in. "Stop the presses!" she declared. "Liz, I've got the most fantastic feature for the centennial issue!"

Elizabeth noticed the folder of paper in Penny's hand. "What's up?" she asked. "Is Winston Egbert planning another attempt to break the world's pizza-eating record?"

"Better," Penny replied. "A wonderful short story that ties in perfectly with the centennial, written by none other than Sweet Valley's own Ken Matthews."

"Ken?" Elizabeth asked. "You're kidding!"

Penny shuffled the papers she was still holding. "You've got to read it, Liz. It's perfect."

Elizabeth picked up the copy Penny had given her. It had a blank cover sheet over the title page. "I can't wait." She smiled. "It's funny, I never would have thought Ken would be submitting anything to *The Oracle*."

"Well, he didn't actually," Penny said. "It's the paper he handed in for his last English assignment. Mr. Collins just brought it in."

"Does Ken know about this?" Elizabeth asked. She knew how protective she felt about her stories and, by the way Ken had acted when she had tried to speak to him about his story, Elizabeth thought that Ken probably felt the same way.

"Not yet," Penny replied, "but I'm sure he'll be thrilled."

"I don't know, Penny," Elizabeth said cautiously. "We had better talk to him first."

Penny started out of the office. "Sure, I'll do it after the staff meeting. If we decide to put it in, we'll approach him on it. I'm sure he'll say yes. We have to move on this fast. We don't want to miss our press deadline. Here, I've made copies for everyone. Read it right away so you can judge for yourself before the meeting."

"That's in ten minutes, right?" Elizabeth asked, looking at her watch.

"Right. See you there." Penny disappeared to another part of the office.

The feeling that there would be problems dissolved as Elizabeth thought of how proud Ken would be to know that his work was regarded so highly. She was thrilled for him now, not only because he had written a good paper and gotten to stay on the team, but also because she knew he had proved something to himself.

Elizabeth turned past the title page and started to read the story. *There must be some mistake*, she thought as she read the first few sentences. She didn't need to read any further, but she went on, sentence after sentence, paragraph after paragraph. There was no mistake: This was her story!

Elizabeth's first thought was that somehow Ken had gotten the two papers mixed up and that he had accidentally handed in the wrong paper. But a look at the title page told Elizabeth the horrible truth. There, in a different typeface, was her title but Ken's name. She couldn't believe it. She couldn't believe Ken would do a thing like this. It was unthinkable! He knew how much the story meant to her, and he'd just stolen it!

Elizabeth started to run out of the office to find Mr. Collins. She had to stop this somehow. As she ran past Jessica, her sister called to her. "Liz, I've got about fifty of these done, so when you can get busy with the felt pen, I'd—"

"Not now, Jess," Elizabeth blurted out. She ran out of the office and down the hall to the faculty lounge. Mr. Fellows opened the door. When she asked for the *Oracle* adviser, he said that Mr. Collins had left a few minutes earlier. That meant he must already have gone to the meeting, Elizabeth thought, which was going to make everything a lot more difficult.

Elizabeth got to Mr. Collins's classroom just as the *Oracle* staff meeting was about to start. Each member of the staff had a copy of Ken's story in front of him. Everyone was smiling, especially Mr. Collins.

He turned to Elizabeth and nodded as she took her seat. "Good. We're all here," he said, looking around the room.

Olivia Davidson, the arts editor for *The Oracle*, was the first to speak. "I've read this over twice, and I'm awestruck. I mean, I've always known Ken was bright, but this is a wonderful surprise."

"It's a perfect addition to this issue," John agreed. "The way the new kid in the story viewed Sweet Valley made me feel really proud of the town."

"We can't publish this story," Elizabeth blurted out. "We just can't."

Everyone looked at her as if she were crazy. There was some laughter and whispering before Mr. Collins addressed her. "Why not, Liz?"

Elizabeth's mind raced, searching for a reason. She knew she couldn't tell them the truth, not without talking to Ken first. This was a serious offense. It would probably mean a failing English and getting kicked off the team and possibly even being suspended from school. "Well . . ." Elizabeth began, "it's always been our policy not to publish fiction," she concluded weakly.

"That's true," Penny said. "But this is a special issue. I think we're allowed to take some liberties."

"That's right," Olivia said, "and the story ties in really nicely with the celebration. I think we should print it."

"It would be a nice tie-in with the exhibition game," John added. "I mean, with Ken being the star quarterback and all."

Mr. Collins turned to Elizabeth. "I don't really see any reason not to print the story. It does have a lot of links to the centennial celebration."

Elizabeth was frantic now. She couldn't let them print the story. But as she looked at the eager, excited faces around her, Elizabeth realized there was no way to persuade the *Oracle* staff not to include the story in the centennial edition. There was nothing more she could say, at least not until she had spoken to Ken. Then it was up to him to turn himself in and face the consequences.

Mr. Collins looked around the room. "Well,"

he said, "if there are no other objections to the story, I think we should put it to a vote. All in favor . . ." Everyone at the table except Elizabeth raised his or her hand. Mr. Collins turned to her. "I'm sorry, Liz."

Elizabeth jumped up from her desk and started out of the room. She had to find Ken right away.

"Liz!" Mr. Collins called after her, but Elizabeth rushed out of the room. There was no time to waste. She had to get Ken to confess the truth. A moment later Elizabeth was heading toward the boys' locker room.

Eleven

Elizabeth waited outside the locker room as Aaron Dallas disappeared inside to find Ken. Aaron had been waiting in the hall when Elizabeth arrived, and he had been more than happy to get Ken for her.

As Elizabeth waited for Ken to appear, there were whistles and teasing. She would have been embarrassed if she weren't so mad. All she could think about was what Ken had done. He probably figured no one would ever know. He didn't expect Mr. Collins to want to put the story in *The Oracle*. Elizabeth just couldn't imagine a way that she could ever forgive Ken.

A minute later Ken appeared at the locker room door. His hair was wet and uncombed, and his shirt was hanging out of his pants. He looked as if he had just finished his shower. When he saw Elizabeth, he seemed embarrassed. "Hi," he mumbled, looking down at the floor. "What's up?"

Elizabeth motioned him away from the door. "Ken, I have to talk to you in private. *Now*," she said forcefully.

Ken nodded as if he knew what she was going to say to him. "Sure. Let me get my stuff. I'll be out in a second." He ducked back inside the locker room.

It was a few minutes before he reappeared. His hair had been brushed, and he was carrying his books. He led Elizabeth to a seat near a window in the hall.

He didn't wait for Elizabeth to speak. It was obvious he already knew what she was there for. "I guess you know about the paper."

Elizabeth had experienced a variety of emotions since she had found out about Ken's stealing her story. At first she had been shocked, finding it hard to believe that Ken Matthews would ever do such a thing. Then she had been angry at Ken for taking advantage of her. Now, looking at the sad expression on Ken's face, Elizabeth felt a strange mixture of confusion and pity. She could tell that his stealing her paper had been an act of total desperation.

Elizabeth just looked at Ken for a while. "Why, Ken?" she finally managed.

Ken didn't take his eyes off of the ground. "I don't know," he said softly. "I know it was a stupid thing to do, and dead wrong, but I was up against the wall, Liz. I just couldn't write a good story, and I couldn't face what was going to happen if I failed. I had to."

Elizabeth shook her head sadly. "Oh, Ken."

Ken looked at her. The pain he was feeling was obvious in his expression. "I'm sorry, Liz," he said. "I really am. I know how much that story meant to you. I feel really ashamed. But I want you to know that after the game . . . well, I was going to go to Mr. Collins and tell him the whole story and offer to write another story. I know he probably won't go for it, and he'll probably fail me, but at least that way it won't be a big scandal all over school. I know it sounds bad . . ."

"It's worse than that, Ken," Elizabeth said. "I just came from the *Oracle* staff meeting, and they want to run the story in the centennial issue."

Ken stared at her in disbelief. "What!" he exclaimed.

"That's right."

Ken turned away from her slowly, but Elizabeth went on talking. "I tried to talk them out of it, but they insisted on printing the story. They thought it tied in so well with the celebration. Naturally I didn't want to tell them the truth without speaking to you first."

Ken sank his head into his hands. "Oh, Liz, what am I going to do?"

At that moment Elizabeth felt no anger. She knew that Ken was truly sorry for what he had done. She wished that there was some way she could help him, but she knew that was impossible. "I really don't know, Ken," she said earnestly.

Ken stood up, his face set in determination. "There's only one thing to do. I've got to stop them. I've got to stop this before it goes any further."

He started to walk away from her, toward the *Oracle* office. Elizabeth wished they could figure out some other way to get around all of this, but there was nothing else she could do. It was all up to Ken now.

Several people said hello to Ken as he walked down the hall, but he didn't respond. Suddenly he found himself in an embrace; Suzanne had appeared, as if from nowhere, and she was hugging him around the shoulders.

"Oh, Ken," she said excitedly, "I'm so proud of you."

"Suzanne—" Ken began.

But Suzanne interrupted. "It would be just like you not to talk about something like this," she said.

"Something like what?" Ken asked, puzzled.

Suzanne beamed at him. "My, aren't we modest?" She stood back and crossed her arms. "I just talked to Olivia Davidson, and she told me that you were just about the best short-story writer in the world. She told me all about featuring your story in *The Oracle*. That's the first time they've ever run a fiction piece, you know. Oh, Ken, I'm so proud of you. I can't wait to tell my parents!" Suzanne hugged him again.

Usually Ken felt wonderful when Suzanne held him close to her, but this time he felt hollow inside. He was getting a headache, and her words were making it worse. He knew he had to tell her the truth, before this went any further. "See, Suzanne—"

She interrupted him. "I mean, if your story's so good, we shouldn't let it all stop here. The county arts council sponsors a young writers' competition every year. If your story is as good as everyone says, you're sure to win first prize."

Ken tried again. "Suzanne—"

But Suzanne just kept talking. "First prize is five hundred dollars, and they send you to Yale this summer for a special seminar."

"Yale?" Ken repeated dully.

"Right." Suzanne laughed. She laced her fingers through Ken's and began walking him down the hall. "Of course, you're going to have to spend some extra time with your studies. I suspect you need a broader base of knowledge in literature in general. But if you dropped football, that would give you plenty of extra time."

Ken finally began to understand what Suzanne was suggesting. "Drop football?" he asked.

Suzanne smiled quickly. "Not right away. Not before the big game, at least. I know how much that means to you. But after that you could quit, and they'd have plenty of time before the season to replace you. It would be perfect if you win that game. You could go out in a blaze of glory."

"Yeah," Ken said dully.

Suzanne wrapped her arms around him tightly. "Oh, I just can't tell you how proud I am of you, Ken. I wish we could spend more time talking about this, but I have to run." She looked up into his eyes. "You're the best, Ken Matthews," she whispered. "The absolute best." She turned and ran off down the hall.

Suddenly Ken realized that he was in much deeper trouble than he had suspected. Now that Suzanne thought he'd written the story, she would be horrified to learn the truth. And not having told Suzanne the real story when he had had the perfect opportunity to do so made Ken feel even worse. When he had written his name on Elizabeth's paper, Ken knew that it was a risky thing to do. But he had no idea that it would have such far-reaching consequences. It had jeopardized his friendship with Elizabeth and was sure to have some effect on his relationship with Suzanne. When the truth came out, Ken knew he would probably be kicked off the football team and maybe even be suspended from school. Ken knew he had to do something to make up for cheating. But what? It wasn't enough anymore just to let Mr. Collins know the truth. Ken had to explain. He had to tell his side of the story. Maybe then he could feel good about himself again.

This thought stayed with Ken as he drove home from school. When he arrived, he jumped out of his car and bounded up the stairs, two at a time.

Ken's bedroom was quiet. He sat down in his desk chair and pulled a sheet of typewriter paper from a desk drawer, then loaded the paper into the machine. Thoughts began to race through his mind. For a full half hour he sat there thinking. Then the phone rang, breaking his concentration. He reached for the receiver.

"Hello," he said.

"Hi, Ken." It was Suzanne. She sounded excited and happy. "A group of us is going to check out the centennial exhibit at the library, and I thought you might like to come."

"I'm sorry, Suzanne," Ken answered, "but I've got a lot of work to do."

Suzanne's voice dropped immediately. "Oh,

the exhibit opens tonight. I thought it could be sort of a celebration.''

Ken knew he couldn't see Suzanne that night. He knew it would hurt too much to pretend that everything was fine. More important, he didn't have the time! *The Oracle* went to the printers first thing on Monday morning. "I'm sorry," he repeated. "I can't make it."

Suzanne's voice took on a harsh edge. "I can't see what's so important, Ken. I mean this is sort of a special thing, and I've already told everyone you'd be there."

"I'm really sorry, Suzanne," Ken repeated. "I'll call you tomorrow. OK?"

" 'Bye," Suzanne said abruptly before she slammed down the receiver.

Ken shook his head as he returned to the typewriter. Now Suzanne was mad at him, he thought. But for some reason that didn't bother him so much. As he looked at the blank page before him, he had an idea. Suddenly all of those random thoughts began to organize themselves: Ken began to type. Even with his hunt-and-peck style of typing, he managed to fill the first page in almost no time. He continued to type a second page, then a third. Soon Ken found himself sitting at his desk, staring at a story—one that said just what he wanted to say. It was about five pages long and contained lots of typing errors and misspellings, but it was his. *It was his.*

Twelve

Elizabeth patted the stack of papers into a near pile and slid them into her knapsack. Usually it was Penny Ayala's responsibility to deliver the typed pages of each edition of *The Oracle*, but Penny's car had broken down, and Elizabeth had volunteered to stop off at the printer's on her way home. The pages were all marked as to their placement in the issue, but it took the printer's magic to transform them into a finished copy of *The Oracle*. Usually it made Elizabeth feel terrific to see that transformation, but this time she knew it would be different. The story—her story with Ken's name on it—sat right on top of the pile of papers. Elizabeth had no choice but to let *The Oracle* print it, although it would forever color how she felt about Ken.

After their talk on Friday, Elizabeth was sure Ken was going to go to Mr. Collins with the truth. She even stayed in the *Oracle* office to see if the English teacher would come in and pull the story from the issue. But Mr. Collins had said nothing, and the story was going to be included in *The Oracle*'s centennial edition.

Elizabeth sighed as she picked the knapsack up. She waved goodbye to John Pfeifer, who was sitting at his desk, and left the office.

"Liz." She turned at the sound of her name and saw Ken Matthews motioning to her from across the hall. Elizabeth noticed that he had some papers clutched tightly under his arm.

"Hello," Elizabeth said coldly.

Ken looked around cautiously. "I have to talk to you for a second."

"Ken—" Elizabeth started to protest. She was certain he wanted to apologize again, and at that moment she just didn't want to hear it.

"No, listen to me," he interrupted her. "Do you have the copy of *The Oracle* for the printer?"

"Yes," she answered. "I'm dropping it off right now."

Ken bit his lower lip and took a deep breath. "Liz, can you pull your story out?"

So that was his plan, Elizabeth thought to herself. He wanted her to just pull the story out so he wouldn't have to face up to it. "No, Ken,"

Elizabeth said firmly. "Not without a staff meeting, and you know what that would mean."

"Yes, I do." He sighed. "But couldn't we just pull it out and—"

Elizabeth cut him off. "That won't work, Ken. There's nothing we can replace it with. Besides, there would be too many questions."

Ken handed her the papers he had been holding. "I have something for you to replace it with, and it won't leave any questions, either."

Elizabeth looked over the sheets of typing paper. "What is this?"

Ken smiled. "Everyone wanted a short story by Ken Matthews. Well, here it is." He tapped the top page, which read, " 'Offsides,' by Ken Matthews." He added, "I worked all weekend on this."

Elizabeth looked at him sadly. "That won't work, Ken," she said. "They're still going to ask about the other story."

Ken sat down on a bench in the hall. "Not after this. Just read it, OK?"

"Ken," Elizabeth protested, sitting next to him. "I can't imagine—"

"Just read it."

Elizabeth sighed and began reading. As she turned the pages, the combination of anger and sadness she had been feeling began to disappear. She still felt bad, but not for herself. This time she felt bad for Ken. The story was very good, but the content was pure dynamite.

When she finished, she looked up at him. Ken was watching her, waiting for her reaction. "Are you sure you want to put this in the paper?" she asked.

"Yes," he answered solidly.

Elizabeth took Ken's hand and looked hard into his eyes. "Have you thought about what's going to happen when the paper comes out? I mean, everyone will know."

"I know," he replied quietly. "I've thought about all that, Liz, I really have. But it isn't enough for me to just admit the truth to Mr. Collins. I have to make up for it somehow. I have to, Liz."

"You don't have to make it up to me," she answered sincerely.

"It's not for you, Liz." He smiled. "It's for me."

Elizabeth stared at him a moment longer just to make sure. Then she stood up and placed the paper in her knapsack.

"Ken," she said, "I just want you to know that this is about the bravest thing I've ever seen anyone do."

Ken smiled at her boyishly. "Well, it's either really brave or really stupid. You'd better go before I decide that it's stupid."

Elizabeth stood up and checked her watch. If

she didn't hurry, she would be late getting *The Oracle* to Mr. Fulbright. She said a quick goodbye to Ken and hurried down the hall.

On the way out to the car, Elizabeth saw Jessica seated on the front steps of the school, talking intently with Winston Egbert, the class clown. Usually Jessica totally ignored Winston, but now she seemed to be paying a great deal of attention to him. Elizabeth figured that Jessica probably needed him to do something for her. Jessica could be as sweet as honey under those circumstances.

"Hi," Elizabeth called, walking over to them. "Working hard?"

"You bet," Jessica replied. "Winston has agreed to take care of the decorations for the picnic, and we're trying to come up with some ideas. We've decided to run red, white, and blue streamers down the trees around the edges of the campground," Jessica said. "And we're going to have a huge banner that says on it, 'Sweet Valley, California. One Hundred Years Young!' How does that sound?"

"Terrific," Elizabeth said honestly.

"Yeah," Winston spoke up, his voice cracking slightly. "I wanted to make an enormous model of a computer out of tissue paper and chicken wire, to put over the bandstand. You know, in honor of the town's leading industry. But Jess thinks it might be too much."

"Well," Elizabeth said to Winston, "you can't have everything. The streamers and the banner sound perfect."

"I think so," Jessica agreed.

Winston nodded. "Yeah, I guess it'll do," he said. It was obvious he would have said anything to please Jessica.

"Well, I have to run," Elizabeth said. "I have to get *The Oracle* to the printer if it's going to be out in time." This was one issue of the school paper Elizabeth didn't want to jeopardize.

Thirteen

Elizabeth sat alone in the cafeteria, looking over the centennial edition of *The Oracle*, which had come out that morning. The issue was packed with interesting things: features on the centennial celebration; articles about the town; advertisements such as the one from the Dairi Burger offering a burger, fries, and a soft drink for one hundred pennies. Lots of things to read and talk about. But as Elizabeth looked around her, it seemed that everyone in the cafeteria was talking about just one thing: Ken Matthews. By this time, everyone knew the truth, and everyone was taking bets on the outcome.

"He'll be suspended," Elizabeth heard one girl say. "That's for sure."

"No," a boy replied. "I bet they'll let him play on Saturday and then suspend him."

Suddenly Jessica ran over to Elizabeth's table and plopped down across from her. She was holding a copy of *The Oracle* and talking excitedly. "Liz! Liz! Have you seen this?"

Elizabeth took a slow sip of her milk. "Jess," she said dryly, "I'm on the staff of *The Oracle*. I usually manage to read it."

"No," Jessica said, pointing to an article. "I mean *this*! This story by Ken Matthews."

"Sure I have. What about it?"

Jessica looked at Elizabeth as if she were from another planet. "It's so scandalous! I mean, listen to this." She turned to the end of the story and began reading out loud. 'He had lived his life thinking that every move he made was for the best, so it was easy for him to rationalize stealing the paper. But gradually, the idea came to him that once he had based a portion of his life on a lie, the rest of his life would be based on that lie.' " Jessica put the paper down and turned to her sister. "Isn't that terrible?"

"What's so terrible about it?" Elizabeth replied, hoping that her voice sounded natural. "It's very well-written."

"Come on, Liz," Jessica said. "Everyone knows this is really about Ken. They all know that there was supposed to be another story in *The Oracle* instead of this one, and at the last moment Ken had that one pulled and replaced it with this one. It's all true."

Elizabeth tried to keep what she knew from expressing itself on her face. "Oh, Jess," she said, "just because someone writes something that sounds true doesn't mean it has to be for real. I mean, lots of people who write mysteries aren't private investigators."

"Oh, yeah?" Jessica smiled. "Well, why did they pull Ken out of practice and call him down to Chrome Dome's office?" she asked, referring to the principal of Sweet Valley High.

Elizabeth sat up in her chair. "When?"

Jessica reached over and took a sip of her sister's milk. "Just now. Ricky Capaldo told me. He thinks they're going to kick Ken out of school."

Elizabeth gasped. "No!"

"That's what I heard."

Elizabeth stood up and began collecting her books. "Well, it's not true," she said quickly. "I have to tell them."

"Tell them what?" Jessica exclaimed.

"I'm sorry, Jess," Elizabeth snapped as she ran out. "I'll tell you about it as soon as I can. Right now, I have to do something." She ran out of the lunchroom and toward Mr. Cooper's office.

Elizabeth breathed a sigh of relief as she saw Ken sitting in the waiting room of the principal's office. He was slumped over in a chair, his hands

119

folded in his lap. When she entered the room, he looked up.

"Hi." He smiled tiredly. "Come to give me my last meal?"

Elizabeth sat down beside him. "Listen, Ken, there may be a way out of this."

Ken put his head back down. "I already considered joining the army, but I don't think my parents will go for it."

"No," Elizabeth said. "If I go in with you, I can tell them I helped you with the first story but that we just thought the second story was better. They'll believe me."

Ken looked up again and patted Elizabeth's hand. "No, Liz. That's very sweet of you, but the answer is no. I've thought this whole thing through. I know they're probably going to flunk me in English, and I know that playing in the game is out of the question. But, believe me, I feel good about all of this. Whatever happens doesn't matter. I know I did the right thing."

Elizabeth looked at Ken for a moment. She could see he had made up his mind, and she knew he was right. Piling lies on top of lies never did any good. Sooner or later the truth would come out, and it would only be worse for him.

Mr. Cooper's secretary stuck her head out of the principal's office. "Ken, Mr. Cooper wants to see you now."

Ken smiled and stood up. He turned to Elizabeth and said, "Wish me luck."

Elizabeth watched him as he took a deep breath and disappeared into the next room.

Ken had never been to a murder trial on the day of sentencing, but he imagined it must be like this. The muscles in his chest were so tense he could barely breathe. Mr. Collins and Coach Schultz were seated on the couch at the side of the room. Mr. Cooper was behind his desk, looking like a Supreme Court judge.

He motioned to the chair in front of the desk. "Hello, Ken," he said quietly. "Please sit down."

Ken sat in the chair. It was quiet for a moment. Mr. Cooper was staring at a copy of *The Oracle*, which lay open before him. He turned to Ken's story. Ken smiled as he noticed the sun gleaming off the principal's bald head. If a nickname ever fit anyone, it was Chrome Dome Cooper's.

Mr. Cooper tapped the newspaper with a pencil and looked up at Ken. "This story has raised some serious questions that we'd like to ask you about, Ken."

Mr. Collins spoke up from his side of the room. "I know this is supposed to be a short story. But exactly how much of it is true?"

Ken looked around and took a second to collect his courage. "All of it," he replied softly. "It's all true."

The room was very quiet for a moment. "I see," Mr. Cooper said finally in a solemn voice.

"No, I don't think you do," Ken said. The sound of his voice surprised them slightly and Ken even more so. He had not planned to say anything, but words just started spilling out of his mouth. "At least, I don't think you understand all of it. The first story was Elizabeth Wakefield's. She didn't know anything about my stealing it. She gave it to me as a model to follow. But things kind of started to pile up. I just couldn't write the story when it was due. I guess I froze because there was so much riding on it. You know, with the game and all. So I panicked, and I typed my name on Elizabeth's story."

Ken paused for a moment. He tried to read the principal's face, but Mr. Cooper's stony expression told him nothing. "I'm really sorry. I know that doesn't mean much, and I'm ready to take whatever punishment you think is appropriate. I just wanted you to understand."

Once again the room got silent. Ken could see Mr. Collins and the coach shifting nervously in their seats. A moment later Mr. Cooper got up from his seat and walked around his desk. "This is a very serious thing, Ken," he began. "I'm also sorry. Sorry that you stole Elizabeth's paper, but more sorry that you felt you had to. But now that it's all done, the question is: What do we do about it?'' He paused and walked to the other side of his office.

The principal turned to face Ken and spoke sternly. ''Normally, you would be given a failing grade in English and suspended for three days.'' He paused and sat down on the front of the desk. ''But I think we have some extenuating circumstances here,'' he added.

For the first time, Ken felt a faint glimmer of hope. He turned and looked at Coach Schultz, but the coach did nothing to boost his feeling. Of all the people he could have let down, Ken knew he had probably let the coach down the hardest. It may have been a failing grade for Ken, but it probably meant losing the exhibition game against Palisades for Coach Schultz.

The principal went on. ''We're all very impressed that you came forward and admitted your mistake in this manner, and we're happy that you realized by yourself that a thing like stealing a paper was wrong. I'm sorry you chose to be dishonest, but I'm happy that you told the truth in the end. What you did wasn't just owning up to a mistake; it was a real act of courage. I think that's worth something. So here's what we're going to do. Your second paper was extremely well-written and would probably have received an A if you had handed it in when it was due. Mr. Collins is willing to accept the paper for class, but he's going to give it a C. I'm sure you understand why. That should keep your grade at a passing level and allow you to play in the game on Saturday."

Ken felt numb. They were all looking at him as if they expected him to say something, but he was speechless. He had come in expecting the worst. He had never thought he would actually hear good news.

Mr. Collins got up from the couch and walked over to him. "Ken, that paper showed that you have some real talent as a writer. I hope in the future you'll try to make a little more time for that." He smiled and extended his hand. "Between football practices, that is," he added with a wink.

Ken grinned broadly and shook Mr. Collins's hand. "I promise," he said.

Coach Schultz walked over and slapped Ken on the back. "Now, get over to the field and suit up. You can still catch a half hour of the noon practice."

Ken almost ran out of the room. He felt as if his feet weren't even touching the ground. He was disappointed that Elizabeth wasn't still in the waiting room. He had wanted to tell her the good news first.

Ken left the waiting room just in time to see Suzanne rounding the corner. He called out to her, but she just kept walking. Ken ran after her.

He felt wonderful, and he had to share that feeling with someone.

Ken caught up to Suzanne and spun her around. "Suzanne, I have to talk to you—"

Suzanne pulled away from him. "I don't think we have anything to say to each other," she said coldly.

Ken was stunned. "But I—"

Suzanne cut him off. "I can't believe how you have humiliated me in front of all of my friends," she snapped. "When I think of how I went around bragging about you, and now, it turns out you're nothing but a common thief. You've made me the laughingstock of the entire school. I've never been so ashamed. I guess what my father's been saying was right all along!"

"Suzanne, you don't understand—" Ken began.

"I understand perfectly," she replied angrily. "I understand that I never want you to speak to me again as long as I live."

"Suzanne!" Ken called after her as she ran down the hall. She didn't even look back. Ken felt as if he had just had the wind knocked out of him.

So that's what everyone's thinking, Ken thought. He had felt so good about how Mr. Cooper, Mr. Collins, and the coach had reacted that he had completely forgotten about the rest of the school. To them, he was just a thief. The whole point of his story was to show everyone how easy it was to get sucked into something like that, but Suzanne's reaction showed that it had all been lost on them.

Ken walked with his head down the rest of the way to the locker room. He was thankful that the room was empty. He had a heavy feeling in his heart as he suited up.

The sun was shining as Ken walked out to the field. The team was running a play as he walked to the players' bench, but they all stopped dead at the sight of him. A feeling of dread came over him. He was sure his team was condemning him, too. It was clear that they felt the same way Suzanne did and they would never trust him again.

But suddenly the team erupted in cheers, and the players rushed to him. They slapped him on the back and hugged him, everyone yelling at once, everyone greeting him as if he were a hero.

Scott Trost finally stepped to the front and quieted everyone down. "Listen up, everybody," he shouted. The others quit their yelling. "Ken, we've all been talking about this and . . . well, everyone makes mistakes, even me." The team began hooting. "But it takes a really special person to own up to it the way you did. We're all proud to be on your team, Matthews."

The cheers erupted again, and Ken felt overwhelmed by the goodwill of his teammates.

"And, if that story of yours is any standard," Scott continued over the cheering of the team, "well, if you can handle the Palisades defense the way you handle a typewriter, we're going to chew them up and spit them out."

The cheers faded away in Ken's ears, and he thought, *I'm back*. What Suzanne had said to him didn't matter. For the first time in days, he felt as if he had come back home. Back to where he belonged.

Fourteen

Elizabeth opened her bedroom window and looked out at the beautiful Sweet Valley morning. The sun was shining, the air was dry and fragrant, and there was a gentle breeze. Everything was perfect for Sweet Valley's centennial celebration. It couldn't have been a better day if it had been custom-made, she thought.

It seemed that Elizabeth had a million things to do that day to cover the celebration for *The Oracle*. First, she had to go to the parade downtown, which opened the day's festivities. Then she was supposed to cover the unveiling of the new mural that Bruce's father had donated to the town. She had already watched the artist put the finishing touches on it. After that Elizabeth was scheduled to drop in on a party for Lionel

Howard, who had turned one hundred years old earlier in the month and who had lived in Sweet Valley for over seventy-five years. Then, at two o'clock, there was the football game and then the student picnic. Elizabeth could barely contain her excitement. It was going to be a wonderful day.

Suddenly the door to her bedroom flew open, and Jessica rushed into the room. She looked frantic. "Liz, do you have any money?" she asked.

"Sure," Elizabeth replied cautiously. "Why?"

Jessica took both of Elizabeth's hands in hers and led her to the bed. They sat down. "You have to loan me enough for an airplane ticket."

"An airplane ticket?"

"Yes," Jessica said, "I have to get out of town."

"What?" Elizabeth asked in surprise.

"Now! Right away!" her twin cried. "I have to move away from Sweet Valley and change my name. I'll let you know where I am in a couple of years, but you can't ever tell anyone."

"Jess," Elizabeth said calmly, "what is all of this about?"

Jessica took a deep breath, then said quietly, "Well, remember the centennial picnic that's supposed to happen today?"

"Jessica, you haven't talked about anything else for days!"

"Yes," Jessica gave an uneasy smile. "Well, there's a slight problem."

"Slight problem?" Elizabeth knew she should prepare herself for the worst. When Jessica was responsible for it, she described anything short of nuclear holocaust as a "slight problem."

"Yes," Jessica replied. "We don't have any food."

"What!" Elizabeth exclaimed.

"I thought everything was going so well. The band was hired, the decorations were all set, lots of people had bought tickets, and there was going to be a bigger turnout than we'd ever thought possible." Jessica took a deep breath as a tear started to trickle down her cheek. "Now we don't have to worry about everyone getting enough to eat because there isn't going to be *anything* to eat!" With that, Jessica burst into tears.

Elizabeth put an arm around her twin. "Calm down, Jess, and tell me what happened."

Jessica began to cry even harder. "Well," she said between sobs, "you remember I called the caterers and got everything set up? The menu and the price and everything?"

"Sure," Elizabeth replied. "It sounded terrific."

"Well," Jessica went on, "I was supposed to call them back two days ago and confirm the order, and I guess I forgot."

"Oh, Jessica!" Elizabeth sighed. "Can't they

still do something? Just sandwiches or something?"

Jessica sobbed again. "No. I asked them, but they're doing lots of parties today, and they're all booked up."

"This is real trouble," Elizabeth said.

"I know," Jessica moaned. "That's why I have to leave town. We're going to have hundreds of hungry people coming from the football game. They'll be screaming for my head when they find out they aren't getting anything to eat for their seven dollars. All that money is going to have to be refunded, and the Sweet Valley centennial student picnic is going to go down in history as the biggest disaster since the sinking of the *Titanic!*"

Elizabeth hugged her sister. "Jess, I wish I could help. Maybe I could get away from the game, and we could figure something out."

Jessica pulled back and sniffled. "No. This is my mess, and I just have to take care of it myself."

"Well, what are you going to do?" Elizabeth asked.

Jessica wrinkled her brow in thought. Finally she said, "I've got five hours until people start getting there. Liz, are you still going to be at the kissing booth?"

"Sure," she replied. "Why?"

"Never mind." Jessica got up from the bed

and started for the door. "I think I've got an idea."

"What about the caterers?" Elizabeth called.

"*I'm* going to be the caterer!" Jessica yelled over her shoulder.

A feeling of dread came over Elizabeth as she thought about her sister's cooking.

When Jessica was taking cooking lessons at the civic center, she had tried to prepare a special dinner for her family. The results had been disastrous. Jessica had managed to give her entire family food poisoning. Jessica, of course, had escaped unscathed. *I hope the centennial committee has an insurance policy*, Elizabeth thought. *If Jessica does the cooking, they just might need it!*

Sweet Valley High's home games were always well attended, but the centennial exhibition game against Palisades broke all previous attendance records. The stands were packed with hundreds of swaying, cheering people. The Sweet Valley fans were usually more than exuberant, but that day they were wild. Many students were wearing red and white, the school colors. Elizabeth looked over the mass of color, the pennants, and the funny hats people were wearing. The members of the cheerleading squad, minus Jessica, were screaming and leaping in front of the stands, and the crowd from Sweet Valley was joining in with a deafening roar.

Elizabeth watched tensely from a front-row seat on the fifty-yard line. Her best friend, Enid Rollins, sat next to her, nervously munching popcorn. "I hope we can pull this off," Enid yelled in Elizabeth's ear, nodding toward the Sweet Valley team, which was just emerging from the locker room. "It would be terrible for Ken to lose this game after all he's gone through to play in it."

"I know," Elizabeth yelled over the cheering crowd. "Our team is good, but Palisades is really something else."

The fans in the Palisades bleachers erupted into wild cheers as their team, headed by Peter Straus, rushed out of the visitors' locker room. They looked strong and confident. The team had won the division championship the previous season, and Elizabeth could tell from the players' faces that they would be tough opponents.

Everyone stood and quieted down as the Sweet Valley High chorus sang the national anthem. Elizabeth tried to catch Ken's eye as he stood on the field, shifting nervously from foot to foot, his helmet in his left hand, his right hand over his heart. When the chorus finished, the crowd let out a deafening roar. Ken turned to look at the stands, and his gaze met Elizabeth's.

He smiled broadly at her and winked. Elizabeth returned the smile.

A minute later Ken and Peter Straus faced off on the field with the head referee between them. The referee tossed a coin, and Sweet Valley won the toss. They decided to receive the ball. The two teams lined up across from each other. The whistle blew, the ball was kicked off, and the game began.

Palisades' team had a lot going for it. They had Peter Straus, who was a wizard in the backfield. They had a wonderful defense and a good offense. They had good linemen, good receivers, and a good bench to draw on. But the one thing they didn't have was Ken Matthews.

Ken seemed to be everywhere at once during that game. He and Scott Trost worked together as one man. Ken's passes seemed to sail into Scott's waiting hands, play after play, yard after yard. Sweet Valley racked up points.

The first half went by very quickly, and at the gun Sweet Valley was ahead, twenty-one to six. Elizabeth and Enid had been sitting on the edge of their seats for almost the entire half.

"I can't ever remember a game this exciting," Enid said breathlessly.

"I know what you mean," Elizabeth agreed. "I'm so excited, I've torn my program to shreds."

Enid laughed. "Forget your program! I haven't

got a nail left on either hand. If the second half is anything like the first, my knuckles are in real danger!"

Elizabeth joined her friend's laughter. She stood up to stretch her legs and look around for the hot-dog vendor. "I think I'm going to get something to eat. Do you want anything?"

"No, thanks," Enid returned. "I want to save room for the picnic. I hear the food is going to be terrific."

Elizabeth gulped. "Maybe you'd better get a hot dog, Enid."

Enid didn't notice the anxious expression on Elizabeth's face. "No, thanks. You can get me a Coke, though."

Elizabeth nodded and made her way through the crowd toward the nearest hot dog vendor. It seemed as if everyone in the whole town was there. Elizabeth's parents and brother Steven were sitting farther up in the stands. She waved to them as she joined the crowd around the vendor.

The second half of the game had already started by the time Elizabeth got back to her seat.

"Look who's here," Enid said as she accepted the can of Coke from Elizabeth. Elizabeth turned around to see Suzanne Hanlon sitting a few rows behind them. She seemed intent on the game. "I don't remember Suzanne having much of an interest in football before," Enid said slyly.

Elizabeth smiled as she watched Ken return to the field. "Maybe she's just beginning to notice the finer aspects of the game."

Both girls laughed and turned their attention to the game. The third quarter was even more exciting than the first half. Despite Sweet Valley's strong defense, Peter Straus led Palisades to two touchdowns.

By the last minutes of the final quarter, Sweet Valley was behind by three points. It was third down, with Sweet Valley in possession of the ball at Palisades' seven-yard line. The Sweet Valley team gathered around Ken to plan the last play of the game.

Ken bent down into the huddle. He was breathing deeply, having just run the ball ten yards in the last play. He had been tackled hard a number of times, and the pressure of the game was catching up with him. Just then Coach Schultz called Ken aside.

"We're just down by three, so I'm thinking of sending in Tim Bradley and going for a field goal," the coach said. "That'll tie us." He turned to Ken. "What do you think, Ken?"

"Coach," Ken said, "in a tie, no one wins. Scott and I have already been hitting it today. Let us go for it."

The coach studied Ken's face for a moment. Then he straightened up and slapped his quarterback on the back. "Go for it, Ken! It's your day."

Ken headed back to the huddle and called a quick snap play in which he would pass to Scott, who would cut left for the goal.

The huddle broke up, and the team took the line. Ken bent down and wiped the sweat off his brow. The most important play of his life was ahead of him. He called the signals, and the ball was snapped.

Ken faded back a few yards and waited for Scott to get clear of Palisades' tackles. But just as he did, Scott slipped and fell. Ken looked for another receiver in the clear, but there was none. Then Sweet Valley's defense line began to break. Ken knew it was up to him to run for the end zone. He tucked the ball under his arm and forged straight ahead. Everyone in the stands stood up. Ken pushed on until he reached a pile of tackled players directly in front of him. He knew there was no way to get into the end zone without making a desperate attempt to get over the pile. Being careful not to lose his balance, Ken ran as fast as he could and leaped off the ground. It was as though he were flying over the mass. A second later, Ken hit the ground running. There was nothing between him and the end zone. In three strides he was over the line. The gun sounded. Sweet Valley High had beaten Palisades, thirty-four to thirty-one.

In the next instant Ken felt a swell of bodies surging around him. People were hugging him, screaming, and cheering. A minute later Elizabeth Wakefield appeared at the front of the crowd. She wrapped her arms around Ken and yelled into his ear, "Nice game, Ken!"

Ken returned the hug and lifted her off the ground. "Thanks, Liz," he said. "Thanks for everything."

When he put Elizabeth down, she was swallowed by the rest of the crowd. The overjoyed Sweet Valley team hoisted Ken onto their shoulders and carried him off to the locker room. Outside the entrance a surprise awaited Ken: Suzanne Hanlon.

"Hello, Suzanne," Ken said softly.

Suzanne looked into his eyes. "Oh, Ken, can you ever forgive me?" She took his hand and held it tightly. "I've been so stupid. I guess I just didn't see how much courage it took for you to write that second story. I'm sorry. Please say you'll forgive me."

Ken stared at Suzanne's face. It was the same face he thought he loved. He looked at Suzanne's eyes and felt himself falling under her spell again. "Sure." He smiled. "Of course, I forgive you."

Suzanne hugged him. They kissed, and she put her arm through his to walk him the rest of the way to the locker room. "Now, hurry up and get dressed," she said and smiled. "If we rush we can meet my friends at the library. There's a history lecture this afternoon, and we can just make it. After that, I've invited Mark and some of the others over for dinner. I showed Mark your story, and he says you're a natural writer. He's really eager to talk to you about it."

Ken stopped. "But, Suzanne," he protested, "the picnic's this afternoon. Everyone is expecting me there. I promised Jessica Wakefield I'd man the kissing booth, and—"

Suzanne cut him off with her light laugh. "Oh, Ken, grow up. All that stuff is behind you now. You didn't really want to go to that silly picnic anyway."

Ken studied her for a moment, then his face broke into a smile. "You're right, Suzanne," he said softly. "It *is* time for me to grow up. To start making decisions on my own, like a mature person."

"Great." She beamed.

"So," Ken continued, "my first mature decision is to go to the picnic."

Suzanne stopped, and an expression of disbelief crossed her face. "What?"

Ken stepped back and looked at her. He could see for the first time that he hadn't ever really been in love with her. He guessed he had been in love with her image. And Suzanne had never really loved him either. He remembered all the ways she had tried to change him: suggesting he drop football; taking him to poetry readings and art films; and giving up on him when everyone else, all his real friends, still believed in him.

"Yup," he said and smiled. "You see, Suzanne, history lectures bore me, art films bore me, your friends bore me, and, if you want to know the truth, I guess you bore me, too. So, I hope you have a wonderful time with all your friends, Suzanne, I really do. As for me, I wouldn't miss this picnic if Shakespeare, Mark Andrews, Ingrid, and Ingmar were all going to be at your house in person." Ken leaned over and kissed the stunned girl on the cheek. "See you around," he said and walked away.

Fifteen

As she looked out over the picnic grounds, Elizabeth felt as though she would never want to kiss anyone again in her life. She had been standing at the kissing booth for over two hours, selling kiss after kiss.

The decorations at the picnic grounds were beautiful, and Elizabeth thought Winston had done a terrific job. The trees bordering the field were wrapped like barbers' poles with red, white, and blue streamers; crepe-paper bunting hung from the lower tree branches. Between two poles from a volleyball net, Winston had stretched a colorful banner that read: "Sweet Valley. One Hundred Years Young!"

At one end of the field, a bandstand had been set up, and on it The Droids, Sweet Valley

High's own rock band, were playing one of their most popular tunes. Elizabeth walked away from the kissing booth as Cara Walker, one of Jessica's best friends and Steve's girlfriend, stopped by to relieve her. As Elizabeth walked through the crowd of people, laughing and joking, talking and dancing, she felt proud to live in such a wonderful town. As far as Elizabeth was concerned, Sweet Valley, California, was just about the most perfect place on earth.

Elizabeth approached the bandstand, listening to the energetic sounds of The Droids. They were in top form that day. Dana Larson, the lead singer, was wearing a red parachute-silk jumpsuit and was prancing around the stage in a near frenzy. Drummer Emily Mayer and bassist Dan Scott were pumping out a driving beat. Although Dan and Emily's romance had gotten off to a shaky start, Elizabeth could tell from the intense looks exchanged between them that things couldn't be better.

Guy Chesney's keyboard playing never sounded more professional to Elizabeth, and the large crowd surrounding the bandstand burst into cheers as Max Dellon began a solo on lead guitar. If The Droids continued to remain in top form, Elizabeth thought, it wouldn't be long before someone in the music industry took notice.

Elizabeth was surprised to see Lynne Henry

standing apart from the crowd at one end of the bandstand. Lynne was a junior at Sweet Valley High, and Elizabeth had never seen her anywhere outside of school. She was terribly shy, and as far as Elizabeth knew, Lynne didn't have any friends. Elizabeth wondered whether Lynne had come to the picnic alone. She was standing transfixed as she watched The Droids play. It seemed to Elizabeth that Lynne was fascinated by the music, as if it meant something very personal to her.

Oh, well, Elizabeth thought, shaking her head. *I'm probably just getting carried away again.* Sometimes Elizabeth's writer's imagination caused her to create situations that really didn't exist.

Anyone who knew the crowd from Sweet Valley High would have realized that one person was conspicuous by her absence. Jessica was nowhere in sight. Elizabeth hadn't seen her twin all day. When Elizabeth had arrived at the picnic grounds, she had immediately noticed the food setup at the opposite end of the field from the bandstand. Instead of hot dogs, hamburgers, and fried chicken, Elizabeth had discovered tray after tray of peanut-butter-and-jelly sandwiches and countless bags of potato chips. Elizabeth had laughed out loud when she thought of poor Jessica spending all morning spreading peanut butter and jelly. No one at the picnic seemed to mind the simple fare. Everyone had eaten his fill, and although Elizabeth had heard some jokes, she hadn't heard a single complaint about the food.

Just then Bruce Patman and Regina Morrow walked over to where Elizabeth was standing.

"Hi, Elizabeth," Regina sang out. "Having a good time?"

"Yes," Elizabeth returned, "but it feels as if my lips are going to fall off."

"I can imagine." Regina turned her head to the bandstand as Dana Larson launched into a new song. "I knew music was going to be wonderful, but I never thought it could be this good."

Elizabeth tried to think how it must feel for Regina suddenly to be able to hear things as common as music. Since she had been given almost normal hearing as a result of the treatments she was receiving, a whole new world had opened up for her. As far as Elizabeth was concerned, no one deserved it more. Regina Morrow was one of the best people Elizabeth had ever known. She shuddered when she tried to imagine what would have happened if they had lost Regina to her kidnapper.

"Well, I'm sorry about your lips, Liz," Bruce said, laughing, "but I'm sure there are a lot worse ways to raise money."

"It is for a good cause," Elizabeth mused

aloud. "But I must have kissed a hundred and fifty guys this afternoon."

From his pocket Bruce took a wad of one-dollar bills he had just picked up at the kissing booth. "It sure looks like it." He looked around the picnic grounds. "It's a terrific turnout, isn't it?"

"Any more people, and we would have had to rent the whole town," Regina replied in agreement.

Bruce winkled his brow and scanned the crowd. "I just can't figure where Jessica is. I haven't seen her all afternoon."

"I was just thinking the same thing myself," Elizabeth admitted.

Bruce put the money back in his pocket and smiled. "Well, if you see her, tell her I'd like to talk to her."

"You bet," she replied.

Bruce and Regina walked away, and Elizabeth returned to the kissing booth. She studied the crowd, but there was still no sign of Jessica. She knew Jessica was embarrassed about the mix-up with the caterer, but Elizabeth thought it would be a real shame if Jessica didn't see how well the picnic had turned out.

Just then Elizabeth heard a voice calling her name in a stage whisper. She looked around, but there was no one near the booth. Then she heard the whisper again. It was coming from a nearby bush.

Elizabeth walked over to the bush to investigate. She parted the branches and found Jessica crouched low inside the bush.

Elizabeth laughed. "What are you doing in here?" she asked in disbelief.

Jessica looked around cautiously. "Hiding. I just wondered how everything is going."

"Everything is going fine," Elizabeth replied. "Why don't you come out of there and join the party?"

Jessica looked at Elizabeth with wide-eyed fear. "Are you crazy? These people paid seven dollars each for a peanut-butter-and-jelly sandwich and some potato chips. After I finished with the sandwiches, I left the receipts for Bruce and ran. I only came back because I wanted to make sure they didn't mistake you for me and lynch you."

"Don't be silly, Jess," Elizabeth said. She reached in and began pulling Jessica out of the bush. "Now come out of there."

Jessica resisted wildly. "No! Liz, let go!"

"Hey, Jess!" Both twins froze at the sound of Bruce Patman's voice. He was standing right behind Elizabeth. "I've been looking for you all afternoon. What are you doing in that bush?"

"Uh, looking for my necklace," Jessica improvised lamely.

"It's right there around your neck," Bruce said, looking a little puzzled. "I need to see you for a second."

Jessica crawled out from behind the bush. "Bruce," she pleaded, "I can explain everything. See, Lila was supposed to be in charge of a lot of this, but she went to New York—"

"Come on," Bruce said, grabbing her by the hand and starting to pull her toward the bandstand. "I want to do this before people start to leave."

Jessica tried to pull away. She turned to her twin and started to yell, "Liz, help me. I'm your only sister!"

In a minute Bruce had pulled Jessica with him onto the bandstand and stopped The Droids in the middle of a song. He took the mike from Dana Larson and called the crowd together.

"Could I have your attention please, everyone?" Bruce said, his voice echoing through the loudspeakers.

The people quieted down and directed their attention toward the bandstand. Jessica stood next to Bruce, horrified.

"First of all," Bruce began, "I want to thank you all for coming this afternoon and making the centennial picnic such a big success."

The crowd applauded, and Bruce smiled at the applause. "Now, I think we're all pretty proud of how the Sweet Valley High football team performed this afternoon."

Everyone erupted into wild cheering, and Bruce had to wait quite a while for them to quiet down before he could continue. "And I think we ought to have Ken Matthews come up here and take a bow. Ken!"

Everyone screamed and cheered as Ken bounded up to the platform. Elizabeth smiled at him as she watched him bask in the acclaim he deserved.

"Ken, we're all really proud of the team," Bruce said as Ken approached the microphone. "You made it look easy to get around that Palisades line."

"The Palisades line was a cinch." Ken smiled slyly. "It was Mr. Collins who was tough to get around."

The crowd broke into laughter and cheers. Elizabeth stole a glance at Mr. Collins, who was at the edge of the crowd with his son, Teddy, on his shoulders. He was laughing harder than anyone.

Bruce quieted the applause and went on. "OK, now I know a lot of you were pretty surprised to have paid so much for peanut-butter-and-jelly sandwiches."

Elizabeth noticed that Jessica had begun to try frantically to get away from Bruce, but he was holding her arm too tightly.

"I guess I have to admit that I was pretty surprised, too—until I went over the picnic receipts. By serving us these culinary delights, Jessica Wakefield managed to knock the food budget down to just under seventy-five dollars. This means that on Monday, we're going to hand over to the Community Fund a check for nineteen hundred dollars and eighty-seven cents, and it's all thanks to Jessica Wakefield."

He stepped back and waved his hand toward Jessica. For a second Jessica looked as though she had received the shock of her life. Then a broad grin began to spread across her face, and Jessica looked as though she had been named queen of the world.

The crowd quieted down as Jessica took the microphone.

"There are so many people who have helped me with this," she said humbly, "I couldn't begin to thank all of them. I'm just glad that all of you were so good-natured about my peanut-butter-and-jelly idea. At first I had thought about having more food catered in, but when I found out what it was going to cost, well, I thought that it just wasn't worth spending the money. After all, this is supposed to be a fund-raiser. The most important thing was to raise lots of money, right?"

The crowd roared, but Jessica quieted them down. "It was at that point that I decided to cut costs and serve sandwiches and potato chips. So that's it. Thanks again, have a great time, dance up a storm, and eat more sandwiches!''

The crowd again burst into applause. Elizabeth watched with a knowing smile as her sister accepted the ovation. As always, despite everything, Jessica had come up shining.

A flash of movement caught Elizabeth's eye. She turned and saw Lynne Henry once again, walking away from the bandstand. Instead of looking happy, however, Lynne now looked terribly depressed. Her head was down, and Elizabeth thought she saw the girl wipe a tear from her eye. Lynne was moving quickly through the crowd.

Although Elizabeth didn't know Lynne well, she wondered if there was anything she could do to help her. "Lynne?" Elizabeth called out softly as the girl passed by.

Her face streaked with tears, Lynne turned to look at Elizabeth. But instead of responding, Lynne started to run off into the crowd. Elizabeth made a move to follow but then collected herself. She had made her gesture of friendship. Elizabeth had to respect Lynne's desire to be alone.

As The Droids began to tune their instruments for the next song, Elizabeth wondered what it was that had made Lynne Henry so upset. It was strange that the girl didn't seem to have any friends. What made her so shy? The crowd began to cheer once more, but Elizabeth barely noticed.

It must be terrible, she thought, *to be in such a large group of people and not be friendly with anyone.* Elizabeth's heart went out to the girl. Then and there Elizabeth made a promise to herself. When she returned to Sweet Valley High on Monday, she would make an effort to get to know Lynne Henry a little better.

Next month the Wakefield twins take a fabulous vacation on the French Riviera in **SPRING BREAK,** *the latest Sweet Valley High Super Edition.*

Can Elizabeth help Lynne Henry overcome her shyness? Find out in Sweet Valley High #28, **ALONE IN THE CROWD,** *available in April.*

EXCITING NEWS FOR ROMANCE READERS

Love Letters—the all new, hot-off-the-press Romance Newsletter. Now you can be the first to know:

What's Coming Up:
* Exciting offers
* New romance series on the way

What's Going Down:
* The latest gossip about the SWEET VALLEY HIGH gang
* Who's in love . . . and who's not

Who's Who:
* The real life stories about SWEET DREAMS cover girls
* The true facts about SWEET DREAMS authors

Who's New:
* Meet Kelly Blake
* Find out who's a *Winner* And much, much more!

Fill out this coupon, mail it in, and this spring your free copy of *Love Letters* is on its way to you. *Love Letters*—you're going to love it.